WITHDRAWN

PRIVILEGED
CHILDREN

PRIVILEGED CHILDREN

a novel by
Frances Vernon

JAN 2 1988
DODD, MEAD & COMPANY
NEW YORK

*Dedicated to Janice Mitchell
and Michael Marten*

© 1982 by Frances Vernon

*Published by Dodd, Mead & Company, Inc.
71 Fifth Avenue, New York, N.Y. 10003
Distributed in Canada by
McClelland and Stewart, Toronto
Manufactured in the United States of America
Originally published in Great Britain by Michael Joseph Ltd, 1982
First published in the United States in 1987
First Edition*

Library of Congress Cataloging-in-Publication Data

Vernon, Frances.
Privileged children.

I. Title.
PR6072.E75P75   1987   823'.914   86-24151
ISBN 0-396-09007-9

1 2 3 4 5 6 7 8 9 10

CONTENTS

'It is the stupidest children who are the most childish;
and the stupidest grown-ups who are the most grown up.'
C.S. Lewis, *The Silver Chair*

Part 1

RED LION SQUARE
1906–1912

CHAPTER 1

RED LION SQUARE
BLOOMSBURY

May 1906

A child was hurrying along High Holborn with two heavy baskets of shopping. She wore a long green coat which had once belonged to a rich woman. She crossed Southampton Row, darting in front of a cab, and made her way to Red Lion Square. At one of the houses she set down her baskets on the doorstep, drew a deep painful breath and opened the door. Inside, it was warm enough to take off her coat. 'Alice!' someone yelled from downstairs. The girl lugged her shopping down to the basement. 'Thanks, ducks,' said Tilly, the housekeeper. 'Mind you hurry up, now. You're to be dressed and to have dinner in a quarter of an hour.' Alice nodded.

Her room was on the second floor. She paused outside the door next to it and heard someone singing 'Speed Bonnie Boat'.

'When's he coming, mamma?' she called. There was a pause. Alice heard rustling.

'Very soon, darling. Do make sure the drawing room's tidy, and see that you take Newton downstairs. He does so hate cats.'

'But when's he arriving?'

'Oh, I suppose in twenty minutes or so,' said her mother. Alice sniffed.

She unbuttoned her patched dress and threw it, together with her stockings, on to the unmade bed. Glancing at the clock, she saw that she had five minutes in which to scan the *News of the World*, and sat down in the rocking chair, her feet tucked underneath her, to do so. She poured herself half a cup of milk and drank it in one gulp.

Alice was eight years old. Her face was sallow and long, surrounded by a thick mat of mousy hair. Her eyebrows were black, arching and thick. She had a large nose and narrow, bright, red-brown eyes. Her hands were delicate and her mouth was full and red. She was so thin that her body looked knobbly even when she was fully clothed.

She finished the most important murder story, then quickly threw aside the newspaper and went to her wardrobe. She took out a frilly dress, a camisole, a linen petticoat, silk socks and patent leather shoes. These she put on with great speed, except the shoes, with whose buttons she fumbled, cursing. She combed her hair, wincing as the snarls caught, and put on a white Alice band. She went to the door and then, turning back, grabbed a coral brooch from her table and pinned it on. She had to walk slowly downstairs because the dress was too tight for her.

On the first floor there was a large drawing room. A fire blazed in the grate, opposite two high windows which looked out on the darkening oblong of the square. Dark blue velvet curtains and heavy looped pelmets hung round the windows. The plaster of the wall panels was mouldering and, although the panels were filled with blue damask, the plaster sometimes crumbled on to the floor. Alice picked up a few scraps of it.

The floor was covered with an Aubusson-type carpet, upon which stood several small gilt tables and a Recamier sofa, which had golden tassels hanging from its rolled back. Louis Quinze chairs were pushed back against the walls and the false doors, whose gilded beading was in decay.

Alice gently slapped Newton, a fat tabby cat, for sitting on the big armchair, and carried him downstairs with her after she had thrown more coal on the fire. She collected her supper of stew, apples and beer from Tilly and took it to the library, where she ate it on the window seat.

Alice worked in the library and her mother sometimes entertained there. The long table was scattered with books, darning and paints. The walls were painted yellow-green and Japanese pictures hung between the bookshelves. The most comfortable chairs were down here.

A cab clopped up to the door. Alice poked her head through the chintz curtains and saw a man in a red-lined cloak get out of the cab. She gobbled the rest of her supper. She heard the maid saying, 'Good evening, Mr Cohen, sir. Mrs Molloy is in the drawing room, sir.'

'Thank you, Bridget.'

Bridget took Mr Cohen upstairs and announced him. Then she ran downstairs to the library. 'Alicky, you should be up there! You know your mother likes it that way. Holy Mary, child, you can't go up with your face covered in gravy. Hold still a moment.' Bridget scrubbed Alice's mouth and chin with her handkerchief.

'Ah, Bridie, don't scold. And let me do it myself,' she replied, reaching for the handkerchief.

'Oh yes, you could do it yourself if you would, but you wouldn't.'

Alice went into the drawing room, and made a pretty half-curtsey in a shy fashion. Mr Cohen was leaning over her mother's shoulder. 'Good evening, Mr Cohen. Good evening, mamma.'

'Hello, darling. Oh, I see Nanny's put on your little brooch for you.'

'Yes,' smiled Alice, fluttering her eyelashes. 'It's ever so pretty, Mr Cohen.'

'I'm glad you like it, Alice.' He patted her head.

Diana held a velvet box on her lap. In it lay a diamond necklace which she had just been taking off when Alice came in. Mother and daughter caught each other's eye.

Diana was wearing a very low-cut apricot silk dress, although it was rather early in the evening to appear in such a frock. 'Darling,' said Diana, 'do go up and fetch me a handkerchief. You know where they are.'

'Yes, mamma.'

'Of course, Aaron darling. I quite understand,' Alice heard Diana say.

On the second floor there was a bedroom which was decorated in the same opulent way as was the drawing room. Alice went through it into a much smaller room where there was a brass bedstead, a chest of drawers and a small table piled high with books by such authors as Bernard Shaw and

Oscar Wilde. Alice opened the top drawer where, among other things, were two sorts of handkerchief: some large coloured squares and some scraps of cambric with 'D' embroidered in the corner. Alice took one of the latter sort. She knocked over an ashtray as she was leaving and reckoned that she had time enough to tidy it up.

In the drawing room she gave the handkerchief to Diana and prepared to sit down on a footstool with the wax doll which was left on the table for her benefit. Diana said: 'Now, Alice, I want you to have an early night tonight. Ask Nanny to give you your supper now.'

'Oh!' pouted Alice.

'Run along, darling.'

'Goodnight, Alice.'

'Goodnight, Mr Cohen.'

Diana gave Alice a wink which Mr Cohen, who was standing behind her as she reclined on the sofa, could not see.

Alice went up to the big bedroom. She turned down the sheets of the four-poster bed, closed the door into Diana's other bedroom, and made sure that there was water in the ewer and a towel beside it.

She paused in the middle of the room. She heard the rustling of Diana's dress as she was leaving the drawing room. Quickly Alice drew the curtains and then climbed on to one of the window seats and waited. She could just see the bed through a chink between the curtain and the window frame, and the gauze inner curtain hid her face from view.

They came in. Mr Cohen shut the door. Alice heard an oozing sound, and then a sigh. A thud indicated the removal of Mr Cohen's boots, and a clatter that of Diana's shoes. There was more rustling, more sighing. Mr Cohen grunted and threw his coat on a chair. The bed gave a great creak, and Alice saw Diana pull the covers over herself and Mr Cohen, who had a shiny bald patch in the middle of his black, curly hair.

Presently, Alice saw Mr Cohen's buttocks heaving under the bedclothes. Diana's cheeks were flushed, her arms outstretched. Her feet formed two points on either side of Mr Cohen's moving legs. Alice watched for a few moments.

The scene reminded her of what she had seen dogs doing in Covent Garden, except that Diana kept murmuring, 'Oh, darling!'

Bored, Alice sat back and banged her head on the window, which shuddered in its frame.

Diana's eyes shot open, but Mr Cohen was very intent on lovemaking.

Alice cursed herself.

Soon, there was no more creaking. She heard Mr Cohen roll over. 'Diana,' he said. 'You're a sensible woman, I know.' Diana turned round, and he looked away. 'My wife's found out, my dear. She found one of your handkerchiefs in my coat pocket.'

'How sordid,' said Diana.

'I can't carry on seeing you. I promised her I wouldn't.'

'Your wife's very rich, isn't she, Aaron? But yes, I'm a sensible woman. I've made a living out of being sensible.'

Mr Cohen heaved himself out of bed and started to dress. 'I can pay you fifty pounds a year, Diana. I will do so.' He paused. 'Sixty, if you like.'

'Sixty will do me nicely.'

'Here's the address of my solicitors. They'll arrange it with the bank for you.' He put the card on the washstand, kissed Diana and left. 'I'll miss you so much.'

'Cheer up, Aaron.' The door closed very slowly. 'Come out, Alice.'

Alice, shivering, crawled down from the window seat.

'Get me a drink. There's some port next door. And a cigarette.'

Alice fetched them.

'Ashtray and matches,' said Diana. 'He's gone off to a business dinner. That's what he was in such a hurry for,' said Diana. Alice waited. 'Oh, darling, you look freezing. Come into the bed. There.' Diana lay back on the pillows as Alice slowly climbed into the bed. Both she and Diana cast their minds briefly over the sixty pounds a year, and the cost of the diamond necklace, sapphire ring and beryl earrings which Mr Cohen had given Diana. Added to the pensions from other men, Mr Cohen's sixty pounds would bring Diana a regular income of three hundred and fifty pounds a year.

Diana Molloy was a tall woman. She had a figure which she could easily press into the fashionable S-bend, and which, uncorseted, was proudly female. She had almond-shaped auburn eyes, a Grecian nose, an oval face, high forehead, a full red mouth and quantities of hair which was between brown and red-golden in colour. Across the bridge of her nose were eight small freckles.

'Have you done this before, Alice?' Alice shook her head. 'Were you shocked?'

'No,' said Alice.

'But it must have looked rather disgusting. He's so hideous.'

'Well, it did.'

'It needn't always be like that, you know.' Diana put her arms round her daughter, and took her head upon her shoulder. 'You're never going to have to make love to anyone you don't want to, Alice. You can be an artist. But I'm a good whore. I can pick and choose a little nowadays.' Alice smelled Diana's musky scent, her warm white skin and her soft hair.

'I wanted to see if you really did it, just once,' said Alice.

'I know. If I'd had such a chance when I was young, I'd be a wiser woman today,' said Diana. She got out of bed and went over to the mirror. She was thirty-two years old. Peering at her face, she saw a line on either side of her mouth, and several fine lines round her eyes. She saw her soft blue-veined breasts as she glanced downwards. Perhaps they were a little too soft and white. She spun the mirror round on its hinges, but it turned a full circle.

'You don't look old,' said Alice.

'I look ghastly.'

'You ought to smoke less. Tilly says smoking makes your skin yellow.'

'She does, does she?'

Diana went into the other room and took a loose, sage-green dress out of the cupboard and pulled it on over her chemise. She took the pins out of her straggling hair and bundled it into a net. 'I'm going to dine with Augustus and Clementina,' she called to Alice. She picked up a necklace

8

which was made of silver and round cloudy crystals. It had been given to her by Michael Molloy just after their wedding in 1896. Michael Molloy had died a year after Alice's birth in November 1897. It saddened Diana that Alice could not remember her father. She was rather like him.

'And Alice,' she said to her daughter, who looked very small in the enormous bed, 'don't do it again, will you? For all our sakes.'

'No, mamma.'

CHAPTER 2

RED LION SQUARE
BLOOMSBURY
August 1909

Alice was in the attic. She held a painting in her hand. It was a watercolour in a new, feathery style which she was trying, and it depicted the London skyline. She was proud of it for the new style made it look more accurate than it was, and she had caught very well the yellow look of the houses on a hot day.

Her eyes were aching from so long staring at the brightness outside. She felt slightly sick, and lay down on the floor. Blue, yellow and pink sun-circles danced before her eyes. A few minutes later, she went down to the kitchen to get an orange.

Taking the orange outside, Alice climbed up the dirty area steps and stood on the lowest bar of the gate at the top. She swung herself backwards and forwards, idly picking off the hot black blisters of paint on the railings, trying to think of something to do. She could only swing on the area gate when Tilly was in the scullery and could not see her from the window.

A fat, red-haired man, in a large apron which was none too clean and a boater hat which was too small for him, was walking along the pavement. Alice stopped swinging, closed the gate and stood behind it with her arms folded on the top bar. 'Afternoon, Mr O'Leary.'

'I want to see Mrs Molloy.'

'Oh, you can't see her today, Mr O'Leary. She's got a sick headache because she's so worried.'

'She's cause to be worried. This bill's been owing for six months.'

'Isn't that a shame now, Mr O'Leary? Let me see the bill.'

Alice took it from his hand. 'Ah, that's shocking!' She frowned and shook her head.

'Let me in. I want to talk to Mrs Molloy.'

'I told you, she's got the sick headache. I'll tell you what we'll do, Mr O'Leary. You give her a month's more tick, like the good Catholic you are, and she'll pawn that lovely diamond ring of hers just as soon as she can, and then you'll be paid with interest.'

Diana had told Alice that she reckoned that the lord who was currently her keeper would be moving on within a month. The ring was a topaz, not a diamond. 'Just a month, Mr O'Leary.'

'She'll get no more tick from me. I want cash down from you from now on. And if this bill isn't paid within a month, I'll have the law on her.'

'Did you know it's against the law to adulterate food, Mr O'Leary?'

'To what?'

'To put chalk in your bread.'

He tried to slap her.

'I'll take the bill, shall I, and show it to her? I'm sure she didn't know it was so much.'

His little eyes crinkled up with suspicion. Alice watched. 'You'd better do that,' he said, and went away scowling.

Alice sighed. She decided to go for a walk.

'And I'll be coming again tomorrow!' he shouted at her.

Alice trudged through the narrow Holborn streets. The day was hot and sticky. The windows in the shabbier houses looked black and very dusty. The smell of horse dung, rotting vegetables and tired, sweaty people was stifling in the heat. Diana had told Alice that summer in the country was the best season of the year, but Alice could not believe it. She imagined the country as a sort of endless Kensington Gardens, and you could smell London there.

She thought of going to the British Museum, but she knew that they would not let her in looking as dirty as she did today. Longingly she recalled the cool, echoing rooms of the Museum. 'I'll have a dip,' she said to herself. She took an omnibus to Bayswater Road and marvelled at the women on the top deck, who were wearing huge heavy hats, corsets, long sleeves and high-necked dresses even in this weather, just because it was daytime. A very small boy sitting opposite her was wearing more clothes than she wore in the winter. His face was scarlet, and he kept twisting and turning to see the streets below him.

Alice went to the Longwater in Kensington Gardens. She idled on a shady path as a gardener walked past and a nanny shepherded her charges to the sunlight further down. As soon as they were gone, she climbed over the low railings and ran behind a willow tree, where she took off her dress and plimsolls.

She groaned with bliss at the shock of cold water round her feet, walked a little further in and stretched herself out in the water, dipping her head in it. She wished she could swim. She had once tried to, two summers ago, and had had to be rescued.

She had to hurry back to Red Lion Square, in order to help Tilly with preparing supper, for there were several people coming that evening.

'You been in that lake again? One of these days the park keeper'll have your guts for garters,' said Tilly. 'Oh no, my lass, you don't peel potatoes in my kitchen when you've been in that filthy water. Go and wash yourself.' Alice stuck her tongue out and went upstairs.

Tilly turned to Bridget. 'You'd best tell her today, Bridget, and get it over with.'

Bridget bit her lip. When Alice had come downstairs and had peeled one potato, Bridget said, 'Alicky, I've got something to tell you.'

'Is it Sean Kelly you're going to marry?'

'Holy Mary, the child's got her eyes and ears everywhere!'

'I saw you kissing him on the area steps last night. But Bridie, you'll not be leaving London?'

'That's just it, Alicky. We're going to Limerick. Sean's got a bit of savings, and we'll be starting up a little shop there.'

'You'll be miserable,' said Alice confidently. 'You don't come from Limerick. You don't know anyone there.'

'It's not so far away from Tralee as all that, Alicky,' began

Bridget, and then she noticed that Alice's mouth and eyelids were trembling.

'Now, ducks, don't take on like that. You'll still have old Tilly,' said Tilly.

Bridget drew Alice on to her lap. 'It's torn in two I am, Alicky. I want to stay with you nearly as much as I want to go with Sean. But a girl must get married and have children, and you know I've been homesick for a long time too.'

'It's selfish of me to cry,' said Alice, and she cried even harder. Fairly soon she stopped, and peeled more potatoes with determination. 'Tilly,' she asked, with a vigorous sniff, 'do you feel homesick for the North ever?'

'Not I,' replied Tilly. 'The Five Towns is the ugliest place in the world. I spent a year glazing pots, and that was enough for me. I'd sooner be anyone's cook than that.' Tilly pushed her small spectacles back on her red nose. She was a broad but thin woman, with greasy black hair.

Bridget was so pretty, Alice thought. She would be beautiful if her face weren't so round. The smell of lemon-scented soap, Bridget's pet extravagance, always clung to her. That scent was the first of Alice's memories, that and Bridget's low Irish voice telling her sinister fairy stories. Bridget had taught her to speak. When she was very young, Alice had seen little of Diana.

An hour and a half later, Alice was sitting on the window-seat in the library. Diana's friends were grouped round the empty fireplace, talking. It was dusk now, but the library curtains were still open and the lights had not been turned on. Alice took off her shoes and swung her legs through the open window so that the first breeze of the day could wash round her feet. She gazed out into the grey square. Soon she felt tears tickling behind her eyes as she watched, and ceased to listen to the conversation, and thought of Bridget's leaving.

'Darling,' said Diana gently. 'If you're bored, you can look bored facing us, but to turn your back is going to extremes.'

'Sorry,' said Alice, and she left the window-seat and came to join the others. Diana pulled forward a footstool, and put it beside her chair. Alice sat down on it. Diana took away from her the mug of beer which Alice was holding, and held her hand.

'I know you've inherited your father's head for drink, Alice, but don't have any more or you'll be having the *vin triste*,' she said, smiling briefly and returning to her conversation. She still held Alice's small chapped hand in her long soft white one. Alice looked for a while at Diana's hand and then she too turned back to the group; but she held on to Diana.

Most of the guests were familiar to her. Standing by the fireplace, with his elbow resting on the mantelpiece, was Augustus Wood. He was about forty years old and produced plays. He was a short, pot-bellied man with a round pink face. The top of his head was bald and the shining bald spot was surrounded by an overgrown fringe of blond hair. He was dressed in an old suit. His collar was unstarched, and his waistcoat was half unbuttoned. His wife, Clementina Wood, who was sitting almost opposite her husband, had frizzy pale ginger hair scraped back in a bun, and her grey eyes were covered with small round spectacles. She was always dressed in tweeds, which she might have worn for shooting had she led a different sort of life. Like Diana she was a poet, but she spent more time on writing than did Diana.

On Diana's right sat Henry Johnson, who was her lover; a very beautiful, dark young man of twenty-seven.

Of those present, only these three knew that Diana was a professional kept woman as well as a poet.

Rose Pembridge, a slim, pretty young woman, was perching on the fender. She wore a mustard-yellow djibbah with an embroidered yoke, which made her look a little sallow. She had spent a month in prison for disturbing a political meeting in the cause of women's suffrage. Next to her sat Leo Shaffer, an enormous, bearded, theatrically dressed man, who was in his late forties and looked far younger. He ran an art gallery, and also painted.

Diana, dressed in a crimson Directoire frock which would have been the height of fashion had she been wearing stays beneath it, sat on one side of Alice, and on Alice's other side there sat a strange man: a protégé of Clementina's called

14

James Bellinger, who was a struggling young actor of twenty-one. He was a lanky man, with big, lightly covered bones. He had a thin beaky nose and unbrushed blond hair. His eyes were large and green and he had hollow cheeks. Alice thought he looked like a wounded knight from one of the illustrations in her mother's copy of the *Morte d' Arthur*. He was chain-smoking cheap cigarettes.

Alice studied everyone's appearance, and noticed the way in which they spoke and moved, but she did not listen very hard to the conversation. She did listen when Diana read out, in a flattened voice, a poem which she had written about her childhood. Diana had told Alice very little about her early life and Alice had presumed that this was because Diana's childhood had been especially unhappy.

Diana's poem was called 'Ignorance', and it seemed to be saying, Alice thought, that the innocence of childhood was a bliss comparable to the false paradise of Limbo to which unbaptised babies went — until the innocence was ended, when it became a torment.

Diana had grown up in a large country house in which, with the exception of one governess, everyone had been kind to her. She had not sensed, then, how bored she was, because she knew no other possible way of life than her own in the nursery and school room. Only after her coming out had she wanted to go to university, to learn about all the things of which she was so ignorant. Her affectionate parents had comforted her, teased her, grieved about her and refused to send her. At twenty-two she had married a man twenty years older than herself, a former Fenian who had been imprisoned for his politics, and who lived on an allowance from an aunt. Her parents, who had violently opposed the marriage, took no further notice of her. Proudly she had set out, after her husband's death, to drown her sorrows in work and to be a true New Woman; but she had discovered, once she was penniless, that her happy childhood had prepared her to be nothing but the most old-fashioned kind of professional woman.

'When women get the Vote,' said Rose Pembridge hoarsely, 'your sort of experience will be impossible.'

'I wasn't attacking the position of women, so much as . . .'

began Diana, but she was interrupted.

'But Diana,' said Leo, 'the fate which *ought* to have befallen you didn't happen, did it? By your own talents and efforts you did, in fact, manage to support yourself by writing — a marvellous achievement in itself.'

'I'd forgotten,' murmured Diana, glancing down at the last few lines of the poem.

'Of course,' continued Leo, 'I quite agree that, with the class structure and the position of women being as they are, the Honourable Diana Blentham, eligible débutante, would — as the penniless widow of an Irishman — become an entirely suitable kept mistress for the men who'd asked to marry her before she fell from grace. But a woman of your stamp doesn't necessarily follow that natural course — and I don't think that you should finish that autobiographical poem with a generalisation, even if it's a wise one.'

Diana looked straight through him and said, 'Yes, perhaps you're right.'

Henry Johnson and Alice were gazing up at her. Diana saw her, stroked her head and smiled at her. Alice imitated the mildly interested, unaware expression which was on both the Woods' faces.

'Unlike Leo, I admire the sense of your poem immensely,' said Augustus. 'It's the form I object to. Why write poetry if you're going to make it as like prose as possible?'

'You love all things purple and complicated, don't you, Augustus?' teased Clementina. 'You just think that all poetry should be versification of Walter Pater's prose.'

'My dear, I'm not so very out of date as all that,' said Augustus.

'But you're not a poet,' finished Clementina.

There was a pause. Diana poured herself a very stiff whisky and drank it quickly. It was quite dark in the room now, but she did not tell Alice to turn on the lights and they sat in the mauve gloom still.

'As I was saying, Rose,' said Diana, 'I wasn't so much attacking the position of women as attacking the institution of childhood.'

'What do you mean — the institution of childhood?' said James Bellinger suddenly. He had said nothing all evening.

'Surely childhood is — er — a physical and mental condition, not an institution?'

'It's not a mental condition,' said Diana. 'Or perhaps it is. It's a state of mind produced by living under arbitrary rule. Parental rule is usually a benevolent despotism, of course, but it's arbitrary, absolute rule just the same, and it creates a lifelong fear of independence. If you want adults to be free, really free, you must let children think and experiment for themselves. If you do want them to be free,' she added.

'Yes of course,' someone murmured.

'My dear Diana,' said Augustus, 'I've discussed this once before with you, I think, and I agree that physical child-abuse is rife and ought to be stopped and that it's ridiculous to extend childhood to eighteen or twenty-one as we do, but all the same children do have to be guided and looked after and surely you wouldn't have some sort of institution doing that rather than parents? Goodness, the things I've heard you say about public schools!'

'I don't have to be looked after,' said Alice. 'Not by anyone. I don't need anyone to take care of me,' she quavered, 'I can take care of myself.'

'Because your mother's taught you how,' said Clementina. 'If you hadn't been taught how to, you wouldn't know how to. Children do have to be guided, because they haven't any experience.'

Alice was silent.

'Alice can look after herself: Alice has experience: Alice is eleven years old: an eleven-year-old is a child: a child cannot look after herself: a child has no experience. Question: is Alice a child or not?' mocked Diana.

'Answer:' sniffed Clementina, 'Alice is old beyond her years because she's been made to be.'

'I feel like a vivisected rat,' said Alice and everyone laughed.

'I do apologise, Alice,' said Diana, stopping the laughter with her apology. 'I really do. And I admit that if you were a little older I wouldn't have been so oblivious of your dignity. I'm afraid these habits persist.'

'It's all right,' said Alice.

'Yes,' said Diana, looking down at her daughter, 'you haven't been shut up in a nursery, you haven't been purposely deprived of experience, but all you really have experience of is a little bohemian circle. It's a sort of grown-up nursery, and I don't think it's a good thing.'

'But I've been all round London,' said Alice. 'Into the slums and everything.'

'You're as much an outsider there as a slumming duchess, whatever you look like, my darling,' said Diana, 'because you can't imagine life on less than three hundred a year. And neither can I.'

'When you say "can't imagine", Diana,' said Leo, 'I think you're wrong. You just mean that you — that none of us, for that matter — have ever lived on much less than that. Very well. But if you just make up an imaginary budget of a pound a week you can *imagine* what it's like.'

'I think,' said Diana, 'that it's very arrogant to say that you can imagine the full misery of living six to a room in a leaking slum when you've never had any such experience.'

'You may be right,' said Leo, 'but then, why are you a Fabian? Why do you believe that such things are evils, curable evils, if you can't imagine these evils?'

'I'm a Fabian,' said Diana, 'because the doctrine of gradualism was specially designed for the conscience-stricken upper-middle-classes who don't want Utopia to arrive until they and their tidy annuities are safely buried together.'

'If gradualism weren't inevitable,' said Rose, 'if the Marxist class war came tomorrow, I know which side of the barricade I'd be fighting on.'

'Yes,' said Diana, 'so do I.' And she looked very polite. Only Augustus gently laughed. Henry Johnson turned on the lights, and they all blinked.

'Well,' said Diana, 'what a good thing we're having a cold supper. Let's go through, shall we?'

'The potato salad must be absolutely crawling with flies,' said Alice, 'I forgot to cover it.'

'Not so loud, my darling. Some of us believe in germs, you know,' said Diana.

For a few moments, Alice was alone in the library with

18

James Bellinger, for they were the last two to leave the room.

'Your mother's a wonderful woman,' he said.

'Yes, she is, isn't she?' agreed Alice.

'You're not very like her, are you?' he said.

Alice surprised him by fetching a chair, putting it in front of the fireplace and standing on it. She looked at herself in the dirty glass above the mantelpiece, and she saw her own reflection, rather than just a face, for the first time. She looked hard and then turned round on him.

'All right, so I'm ugly,' she said, 'but I've got a mouth like hers, and a face shaped like hers.' She scowled and looked most unlike her mother.

'Honestly, I didn't mean to be rude. And you'll be awfully handsome one day, you know. You're just too young for your looks,' he said and he saw her relax a little.

Looking at her more closely, he also saw that he had inadvertently spoken the truth.

CHAPTER 3

RED LION SQUARE
BLOOMSBURY
November 1911

Very early one morning, before it was fully light, Alice was in Mayfair, sticking up posters. Every so often she knelt on the pavement, hurriedly pasted the back of a poster with makeshift glue, and stuck it up on a wall. Sometimes she even selected an imposing front door. Rose Pembridge, who was in prison again for militant suffrage activities, had recruited Alice to do this. Most of the posters just said '*VOTES FOR WOMEN*' but one, which Alice liked particularly, was a picture of a woman and a criminal and a lunatic, all disfranchised.

Alice heard footsteps. She gathered up the posters and glue pot with great speed and hid them under her wide cloak. As she had feared, it was a policeman. She walked past him, rather clumsily but in a businesslike fashion, and, as soon as she was round the corner, ran as fast as she could to the underground station at Marble Arch and went back to Holborn. She had not been caught yet. It amused her to put up her posters in Mayfair, where rich and thoughtless young ladies on their way to balls or to see their dressmaker or their fiancés might see them.

She kicked off her boots in the hall and tiptoed upstairs, for fear of disturbing Diana, who was in the bedroom with Sir Evelyn Reese.

In her room, she took off her clothes and wondered whether to have a bath or not. Next to the window she had pinned up the painting of the view from the attic which she had done more than three years ago. She remembered fondly how inordinately proud of it she had been at the time. She was proud now of how much progress she had made since then.

She decided to have a bath and went to boil up the hot water, for there was no running hot water upstairs; water had to be boiled over a gas ring. The bathroom window rattled, the bath was rimmed with successive hoops of green and the lavatory cistern gurgled and coughed. On a shelf lay old water-warped copies of Fabian Society magazines.

She went down to breakfast in her dressing-gown. Diana and Sir Evelyn Reese were already in the library, where breakfast was laid. 'Got a kiss for me, Alicky?' asked Sir Evelyn, looking up from the *Manchester Guardian*.

'Of course.'

Sir Evelyn was a man of medium height and nondescript appearance, with a bristly, nicotine-stained moustache and red cheeks. He was the Liberal MP for Wigtownshire. He had first become Diana's lover in the winter of 1909, and of all her lovers had stayed the longest. Since Sir Evelyn's arrival, the big drawing room and bedroom, which Diana called the 'business rooms' had been locked up. On Friday mornings he was always very silent, for he had to go back to his wife in the country on Fridays. Today was Tuesday.

Diana was walking round the table in her negligée, filing her nails. Sir Evelyn watched her over the top of his newspaper.

'Evelyn, remember you've got an appointment with your solicitor.'

'Oh yes. Well, I suppose I ought to be off. Do I look tidy enough, Alicky?'

'There's egg on your moustache. And tuck in your shirt tails.'

'Keep me up to the mark, that's right,' sighed Sir Evelyn. He kissed Diana goodbye.

Alice, having finished her egg, was about to go. She looked at her mother, who was standing by the window. Diana was pale, but there were red stains along her jaw and her eyes were very bright. She coughed a lot: she had tuberculosis.

'No, Alice, don't go,' she said. 'Sit down. Alice, you know I'm very ill, don't you?' She fiddled with the ring on her third finger.

'Yes, mamma.'

21

'I didn't know till yesterday — the doctor says I shall probably live for one, or at the most two, years. I want you to go and live with my brother when I'm gone.'

Alice watched the sun drift over the marmalade pot, along the floor and back beyond the window ledge, leaving the room in shade. 'Do you mean that Protestant priest?'

'Yes.'

'Mother of God, mamma, isn't there any alternative? Isn't it bad enough that you may die, without . . .'

'Listen, Alice. Roderick isn't a demon. He's married but he's got no children. When I was small, he was fond of me. Of course, my running off with an Irish immigrant and then becoming a whore prevented him from seeing me. But I know he would be glad to have you. He may try to reform you, as .you can imagine. I don't think he'll do anything terrible like sending you to school, though, as long as you don't rub him up the wrong way too much.

'You see, Alice, I very much want you to have experience of a way of life other than ours. It'll only be for three years at the most, because I've made a small trust for you, and you'll get the money when you're eighteen and be able to live independently. You could come back to London. Roderick would want you to have a chaperone; but still, you could manage that.'

'I've not allowed myself to think that you might die,' whispered Alice. She paused. 'How could you do this to me! How could you!' she screamed at Diana.

'Alice, darling, please . . . Alice, I won't force you. I just said that I'd like you to try it. I think that such a life might take your mind off what you've lost. Perhaps you could go to Augustus and Clementina.' Diana then came out with a fact of a sort to which Alice was not accustomed. 'But he's got a legal claim on you, and he's bound to think it's his duty to have you. Truly, Alice, you might be happy down there. I don't expect you'll find many interesting people, but there is something soporific and comforting about country life if you can get into the mood for it.'

'I will think about it, mamma,' said Alice, with wide-open eyes. She was seeing her mother in tears for the first time.

22

She waited helplessly for a few moments and then ran out of the room.

She went up to a tiny skylit room in the attic. It was whitewashed, and on a small table there was a crucifix, a rosary, two candles and a painting of the Virgin and Child. Alice pulled out her own worn rosary of wooden beads which she always wore under her vest, and mumbled a Paternoster. Then she sat back and looked at the face of the Virgin Mary.

'Holy Mother, what should I do?' she said. There was no answer, but as she watched the flat face of the Madonna and the shadows on the white walls a thick unthinking calm descended upon her. 'I'll think about it later,' she said, and slipped her rosary under her camisole again. It was cold against her skin.

She had a lesson with Mr Tuskin in five minutes' time, and went back to the library, where he was waiting.

'Good morning, Miss Molloy,' he said, pulling at his tobacco-coloured goatee beard. He was a narrow man with a whiskery face, and his hands were always red and slightly trembling. He had called her 'Miss Molloy' even when she was six years old.

'Good morning, Mr Tuskin.'

'And have you prepared the drawing of the Palladian house I set you?'

'Yes.'

'Excellent. I happened to notice these on the shelf, Miss Molloy . . .' He proffered some sheets of scrap paper. 'How long ago did you complete them?'

'A few months ago.'

'Really? What period of costume does this represent, may I ask?'

'Eighteenth-century.'

'Ah — um — yes, I see, the hairstyle. You have added the skirt of 1855, the ruff of 1610 and the stomacher of 1670. Well, well, what variety. However, the figure and face are well done, and you are beginning to shade so that satin may be recognised as satin . . . but, Miss Molloy, the hand! Really, did you not trouble to check with that famous book of anatomical drawings which Mr Wood gave you? And the shoe. She seems to have a foot shaped like a croquet mallet.'

'Oh, for heaven's sake, it's only a sketch!'

Mr Tuskin watched her in silence, delicately poised on the sides of his shoes. He walked towards her.

'Listen, Miss Molloy. You wish to become a competent and original artist. I tell you, praise from friends and teachers is for the untalented.' Alice nodded miserably. 'Is there anything wrong, Miss Molloy?' he said, and came to sit beside her.

'Mamma's dying.'

'And you are worried about your uncle the clergyman?'

'How did you know?'

'You know, Miss Molloy, I have been teaching you for seven years. Your mother and I do occasionally exchange a few words. To my mind, you have absolutely nothing to fear from some overstuffed country parson who thinks he's living in Jane Austen's day. I pity the poor man. You'll frighten him out of his gaiters.'

Alice made no response. Although she had told him of Diana's illness she had shut the reality out of her mind.

Mr Tuskin paused, looked at her blank face and said, 'Come now. Don't let's bother with accuracy and the like today. A little experiment can aid the hand and eye more than practice. Have you ever tried working in black and white alone?'

'No,' said Alice, looking up.

'The effect can be striking. See how the degree of contrast can be as great or small as one likes, depending on the stroke one uses . . .'

Alice watched. Mr Tuskin was a master of such agile demonstrations, but he had never completed a whole picture to his own satisfaction.

After she had had lunch with Tilly, Alice went out for a walk. She went to Russell Square, and saw James Bellinger sitting on one of the benches, his delicate face reddened by the cold wind. 'James!' called Alice, and ran towards him. He held out his arms to her.

Alice had been walking out with James for a few months now. Though she was only just fourteen, she seemed eighteen to him.

They kissed for a long time on the bench. He thrust his

hands inside her cloak and held tight to her taut, narrow waist. 'I've had some marvellous luck,' he said, his eyes gleaming. 'I auditioned yesterday. I'm going to play Polonius at the Criterion. The play's being put on next year.'

'And you only twenty-five!' laughed Alice, and added, 'It's not luck but talent.'

'I have a face which it's easy to make look seventy,' smiled James. 'Alice, let's go out and celebrate. I was on my way to Red Lion Square, actually. I've bought two tickets for *The Marriage of Figaro* at Covent Garden. You can come, can't you? Tomorrow night.'

'Of course I can.'

Alice briefly considered telling him about Diana. But she had sometimes broached a personal subject with him before, and he tended to look nervous and be silent.

The next evening, she dressed with more care than usual in a blue wool dress — the first dress she had had which was not second hand. It had been provided because she had nearly stopped growing now. She put up her clean soft hair in a bun, and put on a hat. She rubbed a little rouge on her cheeks and thought that with it, by the gaslight, she was quite good-looking. If she had been a boy, she would have been very handsome.

She joined James on the doorstep and they walked hand in hand to Covent Garden. Diana was watching from her bedroom window. 'Well, if she gets pregnant she'll have solved the problem about Roderick, after a fashion,' she said to herself. Diana had informed her daughter about contraception, but knew from experience how unreliable it tended to be.

Alice had never been to Covent Garden before. She and James sat at the front of the gods, from where they could lean over and see the three gleaming half-circles below them, and the seats in the stalls. Few people seemed to be listening to the overture. Alice noticed men going from one box to another, whispering to the women there. Everyone was in full evening dress. The doorman had looked askance at James and Alice.

James sat fascinated throughout the performance. Alice liked some of the music, but she could not understand the words or see very well.

'I'll walk you home,' said James when the opera was over.

'No,' said Alice, 'I want to spend the night with you.'

James looked round him, but no one appeared to have heard. He hailed a cab and they got in. He could think of nothing to say. 'Thank you, Alice,' he said at last.

'That's all right,' she said calmly, and kissed him. As she did so, she longed to press her whole body to his.

James's rooms were high up in a large building in Chelsea. Both rooms were sparsely furnished.

'My landlady cooks for me,' he said, 'but she lets me have a kettle for the fire. Would you like some tea?'

'Please.'

They sat drinking their tea in silence. 'I'm sorry there's no fire in the other room,' said James when they had finished.

'I doubt if I'll be cold,' Alice replied, gazing at him over her cracked cup.

'Come on then,' he said quietly, and held out his hand to her. When they were in the bedroom, he pushed her on to the bed and fumbled so much with the buttons of her dress that she had to help him. She got into the narrow bed in her coarse winter petticoat and waited for him to get undressed. He left his shirt on and joined her in the bed. She was tense, but she relaxed as her pleasure mounted. She forgot all about Diana. She wished that he would spend longer caressing her thighs and waist and breasts, but he quickly turned her on to her back and dragged himself on top of her. She waited. She felt a terrible pain, to which he seemed so oblivious that she had to bite him to get rid of him. 'Holy Mary!' she yelled through her tears, 'let me look at it!' She threw aside the blankets and stared at his hard penis, which was blotched with blood. 'But it's so enormous,' she whispered. 'Why couldn't God have made it the right size?' James looked at her with his mouth hanging open, and then he slowly turned away. She laid her hand on his shoulder, but he did not move. 'I'm so sorry, James, but it was such a terrible shock. I didn't know it was going to hurt.'

'Neither did I,' he said, and hunched himself up.

'James, I love you, you know,' lied Alice desperately.

'Try again and it won't hurt me, I'm sure.'

'It would hurt me,' replied James.

Alice lay back. Her fists were clenched. Every small problem she had, and the imminent horror of which Diana had warned her, seemed ten times worse to her than they had that morning. Choking, she left the bed, and sitting by the fire in the next room, but still cold, she could not stop crying as she dressed herself.

James came in. 'Alice, you mustn't. Don't worry about it. I shouldn't have done it. You're much too young anyway.'

'Mother of God, James, it was all my fault! Don't look so frightened, for heaven's sake. I'd better go home now.'

He let her go gratefully, and she cried the more for that as she walked to Red Lion Square. It took her two hours to get there, and when she arrived she was too tired to do anything but sleep, which was what she had intended.

Diana Molloy died on 12 September 1912. She left Alice the proceeds from the sale of the house in Red Lion Square, some wisely chosen shares and most of her books and furniture, which the Reverend Roderick Blentham found a great nuisance to store. Alice left for Dorset two days after her mother's funeral, wearing clothes which she and Tilly had guessed would be considered proper for a girl of her age by her uncle and aunt. Alice had departed for Melton Balbridge in a daze, in memory of Diana.

Part 2

MELTON BALBRIDGE
1912–1913

CHAPTER 4

MELTON BALBRIDGE
DORSET
November 1912

The Reverend Roderick Blentham and his wife Cicely were in the dining room at the Rectory. It was one o'clock, and Alice had not yet come down to lunch.

'Really,' said Mr Blentham, 'one would have thought that after a month here the child would have grown accustomed to regular meal times.' He looked at the clock above the sideboard.

'She's a nice child really,' said Mrs Blentham. 'She does apologise when she's late. And she doesn't hunch up over her food and gobble any more. She's teachable. Only I do wish she didn't talk with quite such an Irish accent. It sounds so queer.'

'She's too clever,' said her husband. 'I fear she'll start petitioning to go to university, as Diana did.'

'Oh, but Roderick, that mightn't be such a bad idea. After all, it might be difficult for her to find a husband. She's so plain and odd, although she might be more like other girls in three years' time. Oh dear, how ridiculous she looked when she arrived, poor child, such a tall unchildlike girl in that pinafore and short dress.'

'If she isn't here by ten past, I'll send her to school,' growled Mr Blentham.

'Oh, Roderick, that would be . . .'

Alice came in. She had been listening outside the door. 'I'm sorry I'm so late, Aunt Cicely and Uncle Roderick.'

'You really must be more punctual, Alice.'

'Well, never mind, dear,' said Mrs Blentham, signalling to

the maid to hand the food round. 'I have some good news for you. Firstly, we have engaged a governess for you, so you won't be quite so bored as you must have been. And second, a relation of yours — I think she's a great-aunt — called Mrs Edward McNamara is staying down here with some friends, and she's heard that you're with us. You'd like to see her, wouldn't you?'

'Aunt Caitlin!' cried Alice. 'Why, I haven't seen her since I was seven. She stayed nearly a year with me and mamma.'

'That's good, dear.'

'Cicely, you never told me . . .'

Caitlin McNamara was Michael Molloy's aunt. She had been very beautiful in youth and, because she was very much in love, had married into the Anglo-Irish Protestant gentry, a class which she hated. Her husband had died in 1903. She had stayed many months with Diana, of whom she had grown fond, but she had returned in 1906 to Ireland and Alice had not heard that she was in England again. It was an allowance from Aunt Caitlin which had enabled Diana and Michael Molloy to survive during the two years of their marriage.

Alice picked at the cottage pie on her plate. She could remember Aunt Caitlin very well. The old lady, who had been born in Dublin in 1848, had told her the whole history of Ireland, from the Protestant invasion of Ulster to the fall of Parnell, and had played backgammon with her for money. Although she was a keen Irish nationalist, she hated the Catholic Church almost as much as the Protestant, and Alice supposed that her anti-clericalism had driven her out of Ireland.

'Eat up, dear,' said Mrs Blentham. 'You must get a bit fatter, you know.' She had been staring at Alice for a minute or more, worrying that she would begin to cry. Alice ate.

'What about a riding lesson this afternoon, Alice?' asked Mr Blentham. 'I want you to be a credit to me in the hunting field this season.'

'That would be lovely,' she said, nodding vigorously.

'The more you practise, the less your muscles'll ache,' continued Mr Blentham, 'and if you want to hunt you'd better get in plenty of practice before the end of the month, when the governess is arriving.'

After lunch, Mrs Blentham gave Alice a piano lesson. Mrs Blentham wondered a great deal about what Alice's life with the infamous Diana had really been like, but when she had tried to ask tactful questions about it, Alice evaded them. Mrs Blentham put this down to a temporary desire on Alice's part not to evoke sad memories. However, the fact that Alice could only play the first four bars of 'Brian Boru's March' on the piano with one finger had convinced her that her upbringing must have been extraordinary indeed.

Alice did not want to learn to play the piano, but she obediently did so. For she feared that, if she once came into conflict with the Blenthams, the soporific effect of the new life she was leading (which Diana had correctly predicted) would vanish, and she knew that life would then become unbearable. Only once had she defied the Blenthams. That was last week, when her uncle had hinted that she ought to become a member of the Church of England. She had simply said 'no', and looked him straight in the eyes, and he had not raised the matter since. She felt that exaggerating her Catholicism and her Irish accent would warn the Blenthams that, while she was prepared to be a good girl, she was never going to be exactly as they would like her to be.

She dressed up in a riding habit to have her riding lesson. It was even stiffer and more uncomfortable than were the starched, pinned, belted and pleated clothes which the Blenthams made her wear every day. She did not saddle her own horse. This was done by the groom and gardener's boy. Alice waited on the mounting block, feeling useless, for him to bring her horse to her.

The groom was a muscular boy of nineteen. He had red curly hair, gentle brown eyes, a fresh complexion and a snub nose. Alice liked his slow Dorset accent.

'What's your name?' she asked him.

'Luke, Miss Alice. Luke Cobbold.' He touched his cap. Alice rode off to the paddock. She supposed that she was expected to make some kind of response when the village men touched their caps to her, but she did not know what.

Mr Blentham yelled at her to keep her back straight, her legs in and her hands at the base of the horse's mane as she trotted, sitting sidesaddle, round the paddock. She wanted to giggle when she saw him stamping his plump gaitered legs in the mud and waving his arms about. He was a bald, short pasty-faced man of fifty, who had thick, very red, very wet-looking lips.

His wife was a blonde woman who had a greyish papery skin. Her nose was always pink. She wore a locket round her neck, and bobbing watch-spring curls over her ears, which hairstyle had been becoming to her when she was eighteen.

'I'd like to go for a walk,' Alice said to Mrs Blentham when she came in from riding.

'So much exercise? Why, the country air must be doing you good,' said Mrs Blentham, snipping her embroidery thread. 'Where to, dear?'

'Oh, just round about. Perhaps over to those trees,' she said, pointing out of the window.

'Don't point, dear, it makes a hole in the air,' said her aunt, choosing a new skein of silk. 'But I don't see why you shouldn't. That's Badger's Spinney over there, though I don't know if there are any badgers in it.'

'What's a badger?' asked Alice.

Mrs Blentham looked up. 'Why, a sort of animal, dear. A rather pretty animal. It comes out at night, and I think it does a lot of damage. It has a black-and-white striped face.'

'Oh,' said Alice.

She went out for her walk after tea, and promised not to go as far as Badger's Spinney, because it would soon be getting dark.

Alice walked along the lane towards Shaftesbury, where she went to Mass on Sundays. She peered into the hedgerows, where there were still a few damp tasteless blackberries and the hips of wild roses. She saw a deserted bird's nest, and wondered what it was until she remembered a painting she had seen somewhere. It was the sky which, of all things in the country, surprised her most. In London it always had a grey or yellowish tinge, even on the clearest days, but here it could be pure blue, a blue which no painting she had seen had ever truly depicted.

Alice wrote to her Aunt Caitlin, and agreed to meet her after Mass on Sunday, and to go back to the place where she was staying for Sunday lunch. They ate with the family.

After lunch, Alice and Aunt Caitlin went up to her little sitting room.

Aunt Caitlin's face had aged greatly since 1906, but she moved in as sprightly a way as ever. She was blue-eyed and stocky, and had thick white hair.

'Well, Alicky, how is it, living with your uncle?'

'It's all right. I'm adjusting to it.'

'Don't adjust too far,' said the old lady, narrowing her eyes. 'Listen: if you ever find it becoming intolerable — and you may do, when all the shock has worn off, for it's not quite two months since Diana died — you can come and stay with me at King's Norton for as long as you like. I'll fight your uncle if you want. I've as much right to have you live with me as he has.'

'I'll remember that, Aunt Caitlin.'

'Mother of God, child, the clothes they've got you up in! Aren't you itching all over?'

'I am, yes,' sighed Alice.

Aunt Caitlin sucked in her cheeks. 'What are they like, your uncle and aunt?'

'He couldn't be more different from mamma,' began Alice. She stood, frowning, in thought. 'Aunt Cicely is very anxious not to upset me. She treats me as though I were about six. I think she thinks of me as a poor street waif. Uncle Roderick wonders how far I've gone down mamma's road.'

Aunt Caitlin laughed. 'How do you feel about the countryside, though?' she asked.

'It makes me feel that I've seen enough of the world beyond London,' said Alice.

CHAPTER 5

⚊⚊

MELTON BALBRIDGE
DORSET

December 1913

'Really, Alice!' said her governess, Miss Rendlesham. 'You ought to be ready by now. Go up and change at once, and then come here and let me inspect your appearance.'

'You really think I'd go with dirty fingernails, don't you?' said Alice, not getting up from the schoolroom armchair which it was her governess's privilege to use.

'You are one of the most insolent girls . . .'

Alice walked out of the room. She dressed herself in the pale pink party dress which Mrs Blentham had thought would pad her out with its bows and flounces, but which in fact made her look taller and more gaunt than ever. Recently, her breasts had swollen. They had sprouted when she was twelve and had remained tiny and conical for nearly four years.

In the schoolroom, Miss Rendlesham, whom Alice towered over, twitched Alice's dress this way and that, sniffing. 'Skin and bone,' she said, poking her. 'No one wants to look at skin and bone.' She picked up Alice's hand and declared that she must cut her fingernails before going out to lunch, a child ought to have short fingernails. Alice slapped her old, yellow face so hard that Miss Rendlesham was sent staggering over to the table and was left, gasping, unable even to shout: 'You'll be on bread and water for a week!'

Smiling, her eyes closed, Alice went downstairs. 'Hurry up, dear,' said Mrs Blentham. 'We can't be late for your first lunch party.'

Alice had only seen her uncle's friends at the Meet during the hunting season or, occasionally, in the village. People of her age hardly ever went out: they were too old for children's parties and too young for grown-up ones. Lady Stopsford, who lived at Melton Hall, believed this to be a problem and held, just before Christmas every year, a party to which those aged between eleven and seventeen could come with their parents. This party had not been held last year because Lord Stopsford had wished to spend the winter in the South of France.

Luke drove them over to Melton Hall in the old four-wheeler. Alice watched the movements of his shoulders and the red hair on his neck. During the winter of 1912, she had made friends with Luke, who saddled her horse whenever she went out hacking along the lanes. In the spring and summer of 1913, Alice was considering ways of persuading her uncle to let her go either to Aunt Caitlin's or to the Woods'. One night, she had gone for a walk round the garden and stables, and met Luke, with whom she had talked it over. He had begged her to stay. Shortly afterwards, they had begun to make love, late at night, in his room near the stables. It was easy for Alice to leave her room by the back stairs, for everyone was asleep by midnight. Though Miss Rendlesham frequently extolled Alice's faults to Mr Blentham, and he allowed her to be punished by being put on bread and water or sent to bed at six o'clock, she was trusted to stay in her room when she was sent up to bed.

Yesterday Alice had told Luke, for whose sake she had already remained at Melton Balbridge for six months, that she would be going back to London. Her uncle did not yet know this.

'Alice, Miss Rendlesham said yesterday that recently you've been very rude to her again. If you can't get along with your governess I shall have to send you to school.'

'It would hardly be worth it, Uncle Roderick. I'm sixteen already.'

'Well, you could go to finishing school, dear,' said Aunt Cicely firmly. 'In Switzerland, perhaps.'

'Nonsense, much too expensive,' said Mr Blentham.

They arrived at Melton Hall, a solid Regency building on top of a hill, where the winds blew cold through the trees which were designed to shield the house. Getting out of the carriage, Alice avoided Luke's furtive, puzzled gaze.

Lady Stopsford received them in the hall. 'Hello, Alice my dear. Clarissa, introduce Alice to your friends.'

'Come on,' said Clarissa, a flaxen-haired, pink-cheeked girl, and she led Alice into a small, informal drawing room where the children were chatting before lunch, drinking lemonade. The girls were grouped round the fireplace, the boys near one of the windows. The youngest sat on the outside of the small circles, not talking to each other but listening to their elders. Alice was the oldest and tallest of the girls, for most of the other girls were Clarissa's friends, aged fourteen or just fifteen. She was glad of this, for as a child she had never met other children, though she had occasionally got into fights with them in the street; she had never had toys, or a proper nanny, or been to school. She was studying other young girls' faces at close quarters for the first time. She wondered at them. Had she set out to draw the face of a girl of six, she would have drawn a face very like that of Lucy Carlyle, who was fourteen, and very pretty. Some of the girls, and the boys, had spots on their faces. Alice had only ever seen these at a distance, and knew them only to be reddish. She did not know that they could be such greasy, oozing, white-headed things. She had always imagined that this was the appearance that leprosy would give one.

The girls were talking about school, chiefly about school-mates who were not present. 'Tom Sanders's an awful fibber. She says she's kissed a boy on the mouth,' said one girl, dropping her voice. 'I call it jolly bad to say things like that. I mean, I know it's not true.' The others agreed that it couldn't be true. The girls called each other Charlie, Luce, Henry, Johnnie. Most of them wore white dresses.

'Where do you go to school?' one girl suddenly asked Alice.

'I have a governess,' Alice replied.

'A governess! Aren't you awfully lonely?' Some of them giggled at the effeminacy of having a governess at sixteen.

'No, not very.'

'I say, where do you come from?' asked Lucy Carlyle.

'Ireland. But I was brought up in London.'

'You're the Rector's niece, aren't you?'

'Yes.'

'But you're Irish?'

'My father was Irish.'

'Are your parents dead?' asked another girl, and then she blushed.

'Yes.' They left her alone after that. Alice thought that they were shunning her because of her background and her accent, and sat stiffly, ignoring them.

At lunch, the children ate at a separate table from their parents. If Alice had been one year older, she would have been at the other table. They entered the dining room in age and sex groupings, but Lady Stopsford had arranged their places at table and had placed every girl between two boys. Throughout the first course there was silence at the children's table. Alice too concentrated very hard on her food. She now had something in common with the others. When the main course arrived, and the parents were quite oblivious of the other table, the young ceased to be polite and talked across one another. By the end of the meal, the sexes were exchanging remarks. Alice remained quite silent. The boy on one side of her considered trying to make conversation, but saw that she was concentrating very hard on the talk at the other table.

'But my dear Mrs Carlyle,' Lord Stopsford was saying, 'don't you see that the Ulstermen are loyalists? They may be a minority, but just as patriots die for their country, so a country must spend blood for its patriots!' He sat back and wiped his mouth with a flourish.

'Lord Stopsford,' said Alice, 'if the Unionists have their way, their beloved country may well die struggling for the Orange patriots, as you call them. Home Rule died with Parnell, and don't you be deceived by Redmond. Ireland will be a free and Catholic and Gaelic country, and the Orangemen can get back to Scotland where they belong. And may I point out that you're being tactless? My father was a Fenian.'

She spoke in a low and clear voice, and when she had finished she started to eat her pudding, while everyone sat quite still and silent. Her uncle's face was purple and Lady Stopsford was afraid that Mrs Blentham would faint. Suddenly, as soon as conversation began again, Alice burst into tears. Mrs Blentham, her face now rigid, got up and took Alice quite gently by the elbow. She bade goodbye to Lord and Lady Stopsford, and led Alice outside. 'Now then, here's a handkerchief. Alice, what on earth can have come over you? Lord Stopsford is your host. Oh dear, what will Roderick do?' she wailed.

'Mother of God, Aunt Cicely, if I'd been thirty years old and rich and if he'd known about my father, as I'm sure he did, for everyone seems to know everything about other people in the country, he'd never have dared puff and blow about Carson and the Orangemen like that, in front of me!'

'Alice!' was all Mrs Blentham said.

Mr Blentham came out of the house and fetched Luke from the stables. They rode home in horrible silence. Alice was no longer crying. Mrs Blentham looked from her husband's face to her niece's and back again.

'Come in here,' he said to Alice when they were back, opening his study door. His wife stood there, biting her lip. 'Go and do your sewing, Cicely,' he snapped at her.

He closed the door behind Alice. 'If you were just a few years younger, I'd whip you!' he·roared at her. 'How could you shame me in that fashion? Not only did you answer your host back — a chit of a girl, no, a *child*, like you — but you actually brought into the open the fact that your father was — was — a traitor!'

Alice ignored this. Her legs were shaking terribly, but she forced herself to look casually round the room.

'Aren't you even ashamed?'

'Well, I'm sorry I've upset you so,' said Alice, 'but I'm not sorry I let Lord Stopsford know my mind. Uncle Roderick, can I sit down, please? I've got something very important to tell you and Aunt Cicely. Please.'

'It can wait.'

'It can't. The chair can't, anyway.'

Noticing that she was very pale, Mr Blentham pointed out a chair to her, into which she sank. He watched her for a moment, and then put his head outside the door to yell: 'Cicely!' His wife came quickly. 'Alice has a confession to make, I suppose,' he said. 'She wishes you to hear it too.'

'Yes?' said Mrs Blentham.

'I'm pregnant,' said Alice.

'You — are — what?' whispered her uncle.

'Pregnant. With child. *Enceinte*. In the family way.'

'How can you be, girl?'

'I had a lover in London. He was staying at an inn at Saddledown and I went out to meet him at night. He was here for about a month.'

'But Alice — when you came to us you were only fourteen,' said Mrs Blentham.

'When I was thirteen I was a year past menarche,' said Alice, 'which is old enough to have lovers and old enough to have babies.'

'Dear God!'

'Right, girl, if that's how it is you can go and lead your mother's life. Now! Go on, get out!'

'Roderick . . .'

'I don't care what happens to you or your brat. You won't get a penny from me.'

'You've got to use the money in trust for me for my benefit, by law,' said Alice.

'Roderick, don't get so upset. Alice can go and have the baby somewhere, and then she can come back to us. It's our duty to look after her. We promised Diana. Alice, dear, don't worry, we'll sort it out for you.' It was Alice's turn to stare.

'Diana! Diana knew damn well that the girl could look after herself according to the corrupt way in which she was brought up. I expect she'll go and have the child scraped out on a backstreet. According to people like that — all the Fenians and Suffragettes and Socialists and Bloomsbury pansies — certain types of murder don't count. Eh, girl?'

'Roderick!' cried his wife.

'For heaven's sake, Cicely, the little tart's heard all the swearing there is in the English language years ago.'

In the end, Alice's proposal was adopted. She wrote to Augustus and Clementina, who sent her a welcoming and sympathetic telegram back. A week after she had told the Blenthams of her predicament, she left for London. Luke drove her to Tisbury station. Mrs Blentham came with her. Luke did not drive away until the train was out of sight. He had hoped to kiss Alice goodbye. He did not know that she was pregnant.

Part 3

BRAMHAM GARDENS
1914–1924

CHAPTER 6

GORDON SQUARE
BLOOMSBURY
March 1914

Anatole Brécu was sitting with Alice in the tiny garden at the back of the Woods' house in Gordon Square. He was hardly more than five feet tall, and had a leg which was twisted so that the foot was turned sharply inwards. He was very thin. His face was pale and small, with high, sharp cheekbones and surrounded by coarse dark hair which was threaded with grey although he was only thirty-three. His nose was very long and pointed. He had a thin, wide, mobile mouth and large charcoal-grey eyes which were rimmed with long thick eyelashes. Above his eyes his eyebrows formed a broken arch. Clementina described him as 'physically repulsive, with an ugly little face crammed with nose and mouth and eyes'. Alice promised herself that she would take him to bed as soon as her child was born. She was five months pregnant now, and it hardly showed. Four months was a long time to Alice.

'Alice, I do not mean to doubt your capabilities, but how are you going to look after your baby? You are so young. It would be a shame in a way, to tie yourself to a child. Children are a lot of work.'

'I shall manage,' said Alice fretfully. 'I might have it adopted.'

'Don't look so frightened, Alice. You could manage it alone, of course. But you might not want to manage. When Liza and Jenny were born my wife ran away. She didn't want children. She wrote for money for a few years. She's dead now, poor woman. But anyway, for a couple of months I had to go out to work and feed two babies with a bottle, and change them and everything else. Kate saved my life then. I was twenty-five, and you are eight years younger than that.'

'I didn't know you'd been with Kate that long,' said Alice.

'Oh yes. She mothered the twins. Now . . . well, they're nine and they can look after themselves and she and I — we just live together.' Alice glanced sharply at him, and he noticed it.

'Did you pay her to care for them?' asked Alice.

'Not exactly. She had just left her husband and Charlotte had just deserted me, so we were flung together. I went out to work and we both lived on the money. But half the money was her right, so you could say I paid her. It was when they were three that she won the scholarship to medical school. And now she is a doctor. She is a great success,' said Anatole. He was a musician, but he rarely finished what he composed, and earned money by giving music lessons and playing in restaurant bands.

'Why did you give your daughters English names?' asked Alice.

'I called them after Jane and Elizabeth in *Pride and Prejudice*. Kate called them Liza and Jenny. I couldn't think of French names for them. I hardly speak French any more. When I went to Russia I learned Russian in two months and forgot a lot of French. Now I can't speak a word of Russian. The same with English. If I left the country I'd forget it all.'

'You're right, Anatole. You've made me think about it. I don't really want it. In fact, it's like a cancer, eating me,' said Alice very quietly.

'I never said you don't really want it.'

'I know that's what you meant.'

'Alice, I did not. I meant that you should only think hard about the whole business before the child is born. No child should have a miserable and indecisive mother. Alice, I will come again tomorrow and give you that book.'

'Will you bring Liza?' said Alice.

'Not Jenny too? Well, yes I shall ask Liza.'

Anatole looked up at the calm, comfortable, dark grey house. On his way out, he mentioned the matter of Alice's baby to Augustus and Clementina. Since Alice had arrived, Clementina had made a great fuss of her. She had insisted on

46

her eating strengthening foods, and going to bed early, and cutting down her smoking, and keeping warm and not walking up or downstairs unaided. Clementina had had two miscarriages and a stillborn child. She was now in her early forties.

'Alice, did you mean to get pregnant?' said Augustus at dinner on Sunday.

Alice paused. 'Yes,' she said.

'Why did you do it?'

'So I could get away quickly from my uncle's.'

'Did you start having the affair simply in order to become pregnant?'

'No. It was for companionship. I liked Luke. And I think he was in love with me. But I hope not,' she added, and frowned. 'I enjoyed the affair. I stayed on for quite some time because of him. Then I couldn't stand it any more. It was my governess who really drove me away. And the alternative to her was school. So I decided to become pregnant.'

'And you thought only of the pregnancy, not of the baby?' said Clementina.

'Yes,' said Alice, and added, 'I was desperate!'

'I'm not criticising you, Alice. What it is to be young!' Clementina shook her head.

'You have every right to criticise me for it. It was a stupid, thoughtless thing to do and God knows I'll pay for it.'

'Now you're talking like a Catholic,' said Augustus with a faint smile. 'Or an ardent Protestant for that matter. The wages of sin and all that.' He paused, and then said nervously, 'What was Luke like?'

'He wasn't a fool. He was very kind.' She thought a moment. 'He was a good lover,' she finished.

'What did he look like?' asked Clementina.

'Red hair and brown eyes. He wasn't very big, but he was strong. He was only twenty.'

'You talk as though he were dead,' said Augustus.

'Alice, we ought to have discussed this earlier, but I somehow — you were always so sure of what you wanted as a child, I thought you would be now. Do you know what you want to do?' asked Clementina.

'It doesn't matter what I want to do. I couldn't keep it. I know I couldn't cope with a baby. I'll have to have it adopted somehow, but I don't know how I could make sure that it would be well looked after and loved.'

'We would like to adopt it, Alice,' said Augustus. 'You know we've never been able to have children. Clem said she wanted seven when we got married.'

'I don't believe you,' said Alice. 'It's just too easy like that.'

'Oh, the wages of sin again,' said Augustus. He put his hand over hers across the table. 'Look, Alice, you want your baby to be loved, and preferably loved by people whom you know, I expect. Clem and I never adopted a child because we've always wanted to know something about the child's parents.'

'Of course you can have it the minute it's born,' said Alice in bewilderment.

'There's one problem,' said Clementina. She put her elbows on the table and clasped her hands. 'I want your baby very much. I've always felt you didn't appreciate it. You'd run downstairs two at a time if I let you. But if you let me — us — have it, I shall never let you have it back, if you want it in two or five years' time. And I insist that if we adopt it you sign a contract to say that you will never make any claims on the child although you're the natural mother.'

'Clem, that's so cold-blooded.'

'No, Augustus, I want it in writing.' Her eyes were glittering.

'You can have it,' said Alice: 'But it's not up to me to make claims on it, or over it. It's a human being, not property, whatever the law says about children.'

'I'll make out a contract,' said Clementina, rising.

'No,' said Augustus. 'Alice, I advise you not to sign anything till the child is a month old. You may fall in love with the infant when you first hold it.'

'I don't have to hold it now,' said Alice.

'I never dared think about it before,' said Clementina, sitting down again, slowly. 'If I had, I'd never have dared ask you about it, for if anyone had suggested such a thing to me when I was pregnant, I'd have killed them. And I'd have grown to hate you.'

'Did Anatole put you up to it?' asked Alice suddenly.

Alice's baby was born on the day of the Austrian ultimatum to Serbia. Her confinement lasted seven hours. The doctor gave her chloroform to ease the pain, but she still felt it. Though each contraction was torment, between contractions Alice could not remember the nature and strength of the pain. In one of the last contractions, she cried: 'It's not fair! It's not my fault I didn't have the last rites!'

Though after the birth she did not remember much of the pain, she remembered the blazing heat of that summer, which ever afterwards people claimed was the most wonderful England had seen in years, with loathing.

CHAPTER 7

GORDON SQUARE
BLOOMSBURY
November 1914

Since coming back to Bloomsbury, Alice had not visited Red Lion Square. She set out from the Woods' house one morning, her insides feeling warm, feathery and empty from a long night with Anatole in which they had made love six times, and suddenly felt that she wanted to see the house.

She shivered a little as she passed through the narrow street which joined the square to Southampton Row, and looked round. There was the house: at the other end of the square. It had not been demolished. She walked towards it, hastening her step as she neared it. She looked up at it.

It seemed so small. She had remembered it as an imposing, if dilapidated, large building, although she had been scarcely an inch shorter when she left for Melton Balbridge than she was now. It had been repainted a gleaming white. There was a brass plate on the door, which read: *J.N. Kettering, M.D.* There were window boxes along the ground-floor window sills. A lace curtain in the window'which had once belonged to Diana's library prevented Alice from seeing to what use the room had been put. The area was neatly kept. The railings had been repainted. As a child, Alice had picked her way along these railings: she would have recognised any chip in the paint, and remembered its individual flavour, the problem of picking it, whether or not Tilly had caught her at it, if the chips had not been painted over. On looking more closely, however, Alice saw that only a thin coat of black had been applied. Most of the chips had disappeared, but farthest away from the kitchen window the proudest picking of all showed through. She could still discern *A.M.M. 1907*. It had taken Alice days to inscribe that.

Augustus had recently introduced Alice to a publisher friend of his who wanted someone to illustrate a children's book which he was bringing out. He could not afford a famous illustrator and, on seeing some of Alice's work, had agreed to commission her. He had specified closely what he wanted. Alice was finding the illustrations very hard work, and the limitations placed on her efforts by the specifications very frustrating. She had no time to paint what she liked at the moment. There were times when she felt that this commission had sapped her of her talent and her energy.

'Perhaps that'll be my only memorial,' she said, looking at her clouded initials. Later on in the war, the railings were to be taken down and melted, to be made into armaments.

'Hello,' said someone. Alice jumped. It was James Bellinger, whom she had not seen since leaving London two years ago. He was in uniform. 'I saw you in Southampton Row,' he said. He sucked in his lips as he tried to smile.

Alice had changed. She had colour in her cheeks, and her narrow eyes were bright. Her eyebrows seemed darker and thicker, her mouth more red, her neck longer and more graceful. She was dressed more tidily than she used to be: she wore a tam'o'shanter, a long buttoned jersey, a straight skirt and cloth-topped boots. A long striped scarf was thrown round her neck. Clementina had bought the clothes for her, because Alice had arrived from Melton Balbridge in the black dress which she had worn at Diana's funeral, and had brought nothing else with her. She looked older and happier and slightly more conventional: she could have been any girl undergraduate, James thought, if she hadn't been Alice.

'Hello,' said Alice, biting her thumb. 'So you've volunteered.'

'Yes, I've just finished my training.'

'An officer, too, I see. You don't do anything by halves, do you?' said Alice coldly.

'I'm not a pacifist,' he said. 'I never was, if you remember.'

'I remember.' There was a pause. 'You look handsome in that uniform. Quite the gallant young subaltern.'

51

'You look very pretty. Where are you going?'

'Just for a bit of a walk.'

'Do you mind if I come with you?'

'Not at all.'

'Were you — remembering the old days, Alice?' he said as they walked along.

'Of course I was. I haven't seen the house since I left.'

'Clementina didn't tell me you were back. Why are you back? You're only what — seventeen?'

'Clem was being tactful. And why am I back already? It's a long story, but mostly because I've had a baby.'

'My God, Alice, why didn't you tell me? Do you think I wouldn't have helped you? Is it a boy or a girl?' She looked very calm. 'It is mine, isn't it?'

'Don't be silly, James. You know I was with my uncle for more than a year. I wrote to you. You don't think I could have given birth to my bastard at Balbridge Rectory, do you? No, I had an affair with someone down there. The stable-boy, to be precise. I was packed off to Clem when I got pregnant.'

'The stable-boy!'

'Oh dear, James, being an officer has changed you! Why on earth shouldn't I go to bed with whoever I please? He was very nice, too.'

'And now you've deserted him, too?'

'What do you mean him, too? You dropped *me*, remember? At least . . . Well,' she continued, 'I have got a third lover, if you must know. An enchanting and adorable and skilled lover. He makes me glow all over.'

'You always were fast.'

'Oh James, what an outdated reproach that is.'

'Loose. Whorish,' he shouted.

'Don't be abusive. When do you leave for France, then?'

'Next week.'

'Have a nice time. Goodbye, James.' She shook his hand and walked back to Gordon Square. 'Oh, Anatole!' she said to herself as she rounded the corner of Russell Square.

James stood in the street, staring after her. His mouth was twisted up.

'Letter for you, miss,' said the maid after breakfast two days later, just when she met Alice in the hall. Alice sat on the stairs to read it. The baby, Michael, could be heard howling in the nursery upstairs.

The envelope was battered. Alice's name and address had been carefully printed on it. It had been re-addressed from Melton Balbridge. *Dear Alice*, the letter began:

> *We are in Belgium. I fought in the battle of the Marne. It is very cold at nights. I have not been woonded* [several versions of this word were crossed out] *hurt, but lots of the men in our batalion have been killed alredy. I am alright really. I know you would want me to join the Army. Their is a Memorial stone at home for the South African War which has something in Lattin written underneath the names, which the Rector says means that it is right and glorius to die for your country. It was put up by Lord Stopsford because his son was killed then. I am sure it is right otherwise Lord Kitchener and Lord Grey and Mr Askwith would not have started the war, but I do not think that it is glorius. It is too sad really. Think of all the orfanned children a war makes.*
>
> *I love you Alice. I wish you would write and tell me why you left so suddenly. You would not explane properly. I have been thinking and I do not like to write this to you, but I think you might have been with child. Please tell me if this is true. I should know, Alice, if it is. I should like to come and see the baby if you have one. I could have married you if you wanted. I would want to. It is my duty also. I hope you are well. You cannot write to me here, but you could send a letter to my mothers house.*
>
> *With love from Luke.*

Alice went upstairs and wrote a letter to Luke. She told him about Michael, what a fine child he was, and how much Augustus and Clementina loved him. She said that if he liked he could come and see her when he had home leave. She would like that.

Then she went back to the breakfast room, where Clementina was darning socks in the morning sunlight. She handed her the letter, saying it was from Luke.

'You can argue with the young fools who go off with their heads stuffed with Rupert Brooke's nonsense,' she said when she had read it. 'But what can you do about that?' She went on with her darning. Alice stood in front of her. 'What could he say, poor boy? He never knew you, did he, Alice?'

She looked up. 'His mother would be so proud of this, if it didn't have that last paragraph.' Alice paused. 'He was so wonderful with animals,' she said suddenly, and she left the room. Clementina wondered whether she was shocked by his attitude, or puzzled, or saddened, or made to feel guilty.

CHAPTER 8

BRAMHAM GARDENS
EARL'S COURT

February 1915

Alice had now moved in with Anatole, Kate, Liza, Jenny and Mr Tuskin and his lover Harry in a large brick house in Bramham Gardens, where the others had all lived since 1913. One Saturday afternoon, Kate was counting out the week's money; Jenny and Mr Tuskin were with her.

'Two pounds from Anatole, five pounds ten from me, one pound eleven and sixpence from you, Christopher — I wish to God you'd do more work sometimes — four pounds two shillings and thruppence from Harry, three pounds one shilling from the dividends of our good socialist friend upstairs, and three pounds from the sale of her picture. Nineteen pounds four shillings and ninepence total,' she said almost at once, and started to divide the money. 'Rent — food — rates — miscellanies. Not a bad week, I suppose,' she commented, in gross understatement.

'I think me and Liza ought to get some money,' said Jenny.

'Count yourselves lucky. You're paid for doing chores, which none of the rest of us are. When you're earning you'll get an equal share. Go and answer the door, Jenny.'

'You are hard on me, Kate. My contribution was hardly less than Anatole's,' said Mr Tuskin, looking bleakly at her.

'You're not holding any back, are you?' asked Kate.

'Don't be silly,' Mr Tuskin replied, in a bored voice.

Jenny went to answer the door, where a large lady in a very high-necked dress and tight-fitting hat was standing. 'Hello,' said Jenny. 'Who are you?'

'My name is Mrs Lyndon. I've come to see Miss Molloy.'

'Oh, well, come on in. Is she expecting you?'

'Yes, I believe so. I arranged an appointment yesterday. Are you her sister, my dear?'

'No, I just live here. It's a long way upstairs, I'm afraid,' said Jenny, who was impressed by Mrs Lyndon's size.

'I'm not so old as all that,' she laughed, and followed Jenny upstairs.

Alice's studio was on the top floor of the house. It consisted of two large rooms which had been knocked into one. Her bed was up there too. With her at the moment was Liza.

'Alice, Mrs Lyndon's here to see you,' called Jenny through the door.

Alice opened it. Mrs Lyndon stepped in rather breathlessly. 'How do you do, Miss Molloy? Isn't the weather simply ghastly?'

'Terrible,' said Alice, and shook hands. 'Were you interested in anything in particular? I only had one piece at the exhibition.'

'I know, but it was the style that I wanted for my new bedroom. We're moving into a new house, in Chester Square, you see . . . oh, aren't you the girl of the portrait I saw at the exhibition?' Mrs Lyndon asked delightedly of Liza.

Liza jumped. 'Yes,' she said, twisting her skirt with one hand.

'Miss Molloy, if I hadn't seen the child I wouldn't have known quite how clever the picture was. It's not only that it was a wonderful likeness.'

Alice was unused to such praise, and asked Mrs Lyndon quickly to have a look round and see what she liked. Mrs Lyndon went over to Alice's easel.

Alice had half-finished the oil painting which was there. It depicted a group of newly uniformed volunteers in the Flower Walk in Kensington Gardens, in the sunshine of September 1914. Two nurses from St George's Hospital were passing them. Children were bowling hoops in the Walk, and their nannies sat chatting on a bench. A faintly reddish light pervaded the scene, touching it with unreality. All that was red in the painting was the mass of brilliant dahlias at the soldiers' side.

'Do you know, Miss Molloy, this painting gives me the

56

feeling that you're a pacifist,' said Mrs Lyndon.

'I am, yes,' said Alice.

'I have a son at the Front,' said Mrs Lyndon.

'I'm sorry,' said Alice.

Mrs Lyndon turned to Alice's table, where there were some illustrations which she had done for a children's book. 'Now those are charming,' said Mrs Lyndon. 'Really very like how I imagined fairies to be as a child.'

'It's what the public wants, I'm told.'

'No, I don't suppose your heart's in it, Miss Molloy, if that's what you paint for choice,' smiled Mrs Lyndon, nodding at the easel. 'I do so wish that the portrait of this little girl hadn't been sold. It would have been just the thing. My husband suggested prints — flowers or something — but I do want something rather different.'

'I did a portrait of Liza's sister,' said Alice, taking it out from a stack of paintings which leant against the wall. 'It's a charcoal drawing, though, not a watercolour.' She handed it to Mrs Lyndon.

'Oh, the child who let me in! Isn't it extraordinary how unalike sisters can be?' said Mrs Lyndon, looking at Jenny's round, dimpled face, sharp hazel eyes and curly brown hair. 'And aren't you twins, dear?' she asked Liza.

'Yes,' replied Liza, who was sitting on the bed reading *Jane Eyre*.

'I do believe a stranger could guess her exact colouring although this is charcoal,' said Mrs Lyndon. 'What a pert child she must be!' And she gave a peal of laughter.

'You could say that,' replied Alice.

Mrs Lyndon looked at a few other things, but decided on the drawing of Jenny. 'How much do you want for it, Miss Molloy?'

'How much would you pay for it?'

'Would five pounds be enough?'

'Five pounds?' said Alice, and closed her mouth again quickly. 'Quite enough, thank you.'

'I believe it'll prove to be quite an investment,' said Mrs Lyndon, handing her a small deposit at Alice's request and promising to send someone over to collect the picture in the morning.

'How silly she was not to like the painting of the soldiers,' said Liza, going over to it.

'She was observant about it,' said Alice, smoothing the five-pound note, 'but it didn't suit her politics.'

'How long do you think the war will last?' Liza asked, turning to her.

'I can't tell,' Alice replied. 'There's never been such a war. It's stuck fast, you see. They sit in the trenches and rot, and shoot at each other once in a while. God knows what the generals will do. If the Easterners' plan works, the war should end quite quickly, but if not, who knows?'

'Suppose the Germans win? Will they conquer us?'

'I don't see why they'd bother. You've been reading the yellow press, Liza.'

'I've never read such a good book as this,' said Liza, looking at *Jane Eyre*. 'It makes you cry with anger at what they can do to children.'

Liza went to put the kettle on and fetched the digestive biscuits. At that moment, Anatole came in. He had just arrived back from giving a music lesson.

'Why, oh why, must the bourgeoisie insist on their fat, tone-deaf little girls learning to play the piano? Tell me, is it still considered ladylike to thump out some dull little air after dinner? Do they really think that it shows their daughters up in the best possible light?'

'Poor Monsieur Anatole,' said Alice with a smile.

He threw off the tailcoat which he wore for giving lessons. It was far too big for him, like the rest of his clothes, which were all second-hand. He took Alice's hands in his and looked up at her, adoringly.

'Liza and I are going to have tea,' she said.

'That can wait,' he replied.

'Can it?'

Liza slipped out of the door and ran downstairs. She knew very well the gleam which she had seen in Alice's eyes. Once, two years ago this coming summer, she had seen Anatole and Kate making love. They had not been in the bed, but on top of it. She had caught a glimpse of their naked bodies. There were black hairs all over Anatole's. She had seen his hard, reddish genitals, and run quickly away. Over the last two years, those genitals had grown to an enormous size in her mind. She had never let Anatole touch her since then. She imagined his hands on Alice's slender body. When Alice tied her hair back with a black ribbon, she looked like a handsome boy in an eighteenth-century portrait, a boy without that ghastly deformity between his legs. Though the thought of the male body made Liza shudder, it made her realise also that however plain she was with her pale hair, thick whitish eyebrows, chapped lips, and round heavy-lidded grey eyes, she was more aesthetically pleasing than any male.

Anatole laid his head on Alice's shoulder, and curled up so that his body fitted into the curve of hers. 'It is with you that I have the greatest sexual pleasure I have ever had,' he said.

'That's saying a lot,' said Alice.

Anatole paused. 'Alice,' he said, 'have you slept with anyone else since you were with me? As a matter of interest.'

'No. And what's it to you if I have? We both believe in free love, don't we?'

'Yes, of course. Have you wanted to sleep with anyone else?'

'No I have not. Holy Mary, Anatole, you're not my confessor, you know. Stop asking me these things.'

'Why are you cross? Is it because you're not sure?'

'Don't be stupid. Listen. I love you and I haven't really wanted anyone else since I met you. But I think that my feelings are my own business unless I choose to talk about them with you.'

Anatole stopped stroking Alice's thigh and rolled over. 'You know,' he said, 'I think that as we have been faithful to each other for a year now, we might get married.'

'Well!' said Alice, 'what a way to propose, with your back turned towards me.'

'I have my back towards you because I know my proposal will be unwelcome.'

'Now why are you sounding so self-pitying? You've got me to live with, and I love you, and what more could you want from marriage? I should be the one wanting marriage. I'm supposed to be a Catholic . . . I've never known a happy marriage,' she continued, 'except the Woods'. And my parents, but they were only married two years. Oh, Anatole, stop sulking and face me. I don't know why you're sulking; I'm only disagreeing with you. That's not a crime.'

She paused.

'Perhaps that's it,' she said, 'I've never disagreed with you at all before, have I, although I do call myself an independent woman. Why do you want to marry me, Anatole? You've had one disastrous marriage, and why did you marry Charlotte anyway? Can I ask some difficult questions now?' she teased, and he responded. He turned back to face her.

'I married her,' he said, 'because I'd made a little money at that time, and I'd spent all my life either making love for money, or having brief, stormy affairs, or sleeping the odd night with various easy-going ladies. I wanted a pretty, sweet girl like Charlotte to care for and make happy. And I wanted her to do the same for me. Perhaps it would have worked if I hadn't lost my little fortune in a bad speculation. One needs money above all things to support that kind of marriage.'

'A thoroughly Victorian ideal,' said Alice.

'Yes, I admit it.'

'It's a pretty ideal, I know, but you can't think you'd ever have that with me?'

'No, of course I don't. I don't know what I want with you exactly. I only want you to — to belong to me. Metaphorically speaking.'

'Well, so do I want to belong to you — and let me add that I want you to belong to me! That's a slightly different thing, you know. But I don't want to make you my lord and master in law. I'm sure I'm married in the sight of God so long as you and I regard each other — as — as spouses.'

'That sounds like a rather Protestant notion to me.'

They both laughed and then were silent and soon they made love again. Afterwards Alice pulled herself out of bed and went to close the curtains. Stumbling through the cold blue dusk to the other side of the studio, she went to light the oil lamp, and then hurried back to bed.

'Welcome back,' said Anatole. They both watched the yellow glare of the lamp on the far side of the studio.

'After the war,' said Anatole, 'we must have the top two floors electrified. It's quite a deprivation nowadays to be without electric light.'

'Yes,' said Alice, 'it doesn't seem worth doing that sort of thing when the house may be blown to smithereens any day of the week. I like my oil lamp, though. There was no gaslight in my room at home. Mamma always liked oil lamps . . . though we did put electric light in the big rooms,' she mused. 'It made us look more prosperous.'

'My love,' said Anatole, 'wouldn't you like to have a baby, now that we do seem to be attached to each other?'

'You sound as though you're afraid to use the word ''love'' to me,' said Alice.

'Of course I love you.'

'Good.' She squeezed his hand. 'Now, I've told you, darling, that if I do get pregnant in spite of being careful I won't do anything silly and dangerous and in time I will get pregnant, I'm sure. You can never be certain about these so-called contraceptives.'

'You've been very successful with the wretched things you use so far.'

'I've just been lucky. Oh, darling, for God's sake don't let's spoil this by talking about it. We've talked about it all before.'

Very soon they got up and dressed. Alice went down to Liza's small, bare, tidy room, which was hung with cheap reproductions of Pre-Raphaelite pictures.

'Let's have some tea now,' said Alice.

'No,' said Liza, 'I'm not going to have tea with you. You smell of Anatole.'

'That's an odd thing to say,' said Alice.

'I hate bodies,' said Liza.

'And you like books,' said Alice.

'Yes,' said Liza.

'Even books that are about bodies.'

'What?' said Liza.

'Well, *Jane Eyre*'s a love story, and love stories are really about bodies. Sex.'

'Yes, but it's not the same as you and Anatole messing about upstairs making my ceiling creak.'

Alice began to laugh and then she saw that Liza looked almost angry.

'In a book,' continued Liza, 'things are as you want them to be. If you don't want to read about money and dirt and quarrels, you don't have to.'

'Day-dreamer,' said Alice. 'You sound as though life's treated you very badly.'

'It's just that — just that I don't like *doing* things,' said Liza.

'Well, you day-dream then,' said Alice. 'I've got to go and be Kate's kitchenmaid.'

'By the way,' she added from the doorway, 'could you model for me again next week, after school? I can't manage this week, I'm behind with those damned illustrations already.'

'Yes, all right.'

'And I'll have to go up to Bloomsbury to get a new fine sable brush. Jenny ruined my best fine brush by painting patterns on her new boots with it, did I tell you? She managed to ruin the brush and her boots and the floor all in one go. I could have spanked her!'

'Jenny's always doing things,' said Liza and she picked up her book again.

Alice ran downstairs to the kitchen.

'Where've you been?' said Kate. 'You know we've got to eat at seven tonight because Harry's going out. We'll never be ready in time.'

'I'm sorry,' said Alice.

Kate pushed a chopping board and five large onions over to her. 'Dice them properly,' she said. Alice sighed, and started to peel the onions, which made her cry. She watched Kate chopping up meat very briskly, a sight which always made Alice feel slightly sick. Suddenly she realised that she was not crying only because she was chopping onions. Kate looked at her.

'Why, you're crying,' she said.

'It's the onions,' said Alice, hunching her shoulders.

'No, it's not, or your mouth wouldn't be crumpled up like that. Now come on, Alice, either stop it or tell me what's wrong.'

Alice stopped crying briefly and shouted: 'Why do you dislike me?'

'Don't be silly, I don't dislike you, what I dislike is the fact that you're making Anatole unhappy and he's so in love with you.'

'Oh, I see, you don't like him being in love with me, although you stopped sleeping together before I even came back to town!'

'How can you deliberately misinterpret what I said, just so that you can have a fight?' said Kate. 'I suppose that's the reason; you quite like quarrels, don't you? Well, I don't and I'm not going to quarrel with you.'

Kate looked at Alice. She saw her young, smooth, long neck, which was lovely even now when there was a lump quavering in it; her adolescent body and strong, dark, angry but unworried eyes. Kate was thirty-one, and her flesh was beginning to sag. Though her hair was still black, lines had appeared on her broad brown face. She had lived with Anatole for eight years and he had never wanted to marry her. She had not wanted to marry him either, but this, she thought as she watched Alice, was irrelevant.

'You're such a blind, selfish child that you don't even know why you're making him so miserable, do you? Well, I'll tell you.' said Kate. 'He's told you, but you haven't listened. He wants to marry you and have children by you, but you won't give him either of those things, though you say you love him. I call it wicked. Can't you ever put yourself out for someone else? For someone you love?'

'No, not if it means having another damned baby!' shouted Alice. 'Not yet. I've got my own life to lead,' she added more quietly.

'But you do love Anatole.'

'Yes, I do.'

'I forget you're still a child,' said Kate. 'I shouldn't have been so harsh on you.'

'I am not a child. I'm a grown woman. I've had a baby already to prove it. But I tell you, I won't have another one yet, if I can help it.'

'It wasn't very kind to Michael to have him purely so as to show your uncle and aunt that you weren't a child, was it?'

'That wasn't the only reason. Oh, leave me alone and stop making me feel guilty!'

'I wish you just knew what it's like to be barren,' hissed Kate. 'I tried so hard . . .'

'Be quiet.'

'I'm sorry, that was a dirty thing to say.'

'I dare say I am selfish,' said Alice after a pause, and Kate said nothing.

They carried on cutting up vegetables in silence for a while.

'I'm going to France,' said Kate.

'What, to work, you mean?'

'Yes, of course I do. I wouldn't be going to Aix-les-Bains at this time of year, you know.'

'I thought they had army doctors.'

'Oh, they want woman doctors now, right enough. They won't turn down my services.'

'Enjoy yourself, then.'

'You ought to nurse.'

'Well, I'm just not going to. I've got my work and I'd be a terrible nurse, I'm sure. And I couldn't if I had a baby anyway.'

Kate smiled very slightly.

CHAPTER 9

BRAMHAM GARDENS
EARL'S COURT
June 1916

Alice was eight months pregnant with Anatole's child. She knew now that Luke and James Bellinger had both been killed, Luke at Gallipoli and James on the Western Front. Re-reading the descriptions of the war which Kate gave in her letters, Alice had cried for them, although she had not loved them.

Liza came into the kitchen, where Alice was drinking tea and reading the paper.

'Really, Miss Molloy, in your condition you ought to eat more,' Mr Tuskin was lecturing her.

'Don't fuss, Mr Tuskin.'

'Alice, will you walk to school with me?' asked Liza. It was half past eight.

'Of course,' Alice replied. Alice took a stick with her, because Anatole and Mr Tuskin were both convinced that this would make it safer for her to walk outside. She felt very comfortable in this pregnancy, and went easily along with the household's insistences on how she should behave.

Augustus and Clementina were living with them now; recently Augustus had lost a great deal of money, and he had been forced to sell the house in Gordon Square. Looking at Michael, who was now two years old, Alice thought that he had never seemed to be hers even when he was in her womb. He had come to resemble his adoptive parents in a remarkable way; he even had blue eyes like Augustus, and ginger hair like Clementina.

Liza's school, which was an endowed progressive school for girls under the age of fourteen, was in South Kensington.

Jenny was there too. Alice and Liza walked through the small white streets and squares south of the dusty Old Brompton Road.

'Alice, do you want a boy?' asked Liza.

'No, a girl. Certainly a girl. My own daughter,' she said.

Liza ran a little way ahead. She swung herself round a lamp post, and her skirt twisted up round her long, thin, black-clad legs. Alice watched her. Liza's hair had gained a little colour recently, and now could be called blonde. The sun had taken away the bluish look which her tight skin had in the winter. Her skin had to be protected from even a weak sun, however, and she always wore a wide battered hat which was held under her chin with elastic.

'I wish I'd had a sister,' Alice said to her. 'A younger sister.'

'Oh, Alice, you couldn't wish for anything so awful!' said Liza. 'People think Jenny and I ought to be close because we're twins, but how could we be, when we're so different? Jenny likes arguing and quarrelling. She's always joking and teasing. I'll never, ever understand her.'

'Sometimes she's as serious as you are,' said Alice.

They had reached the school. Girls, aged between five and fourteen, were running about on the lawn outside the large white house. The grass was worn bare by their feet. The smallest girls wore pinafores, the older ones short dresses with wide belts round their hips. Several were in mourning. Liza opened the gate and went in. She walked straight up the path into the building, greeting no one as she went. She looked odd amongst the others, in her long skirt and old, loose shirt.

Alice stood awhile, watching the girls on the lawn. A few of the older girls were plump or had spots, but most of them had an ethereal look, perhaps because they were growing so fast. Their early youth gave to some of them, Alice reflected as she watched the laughing pale faces and lanky legs, a charm which they would never have again. By the time their parents considered them old enough to enjoy their beauty, the beauty might well be gone. Alice leaned on the railings, looking at their gleaming hair and tiny poking breasts, until the bell rang and the girls started to troop indoors. At that moment, Jenny

66

ran up puffing, dropped her boots and hastily put on shoes over her filthy bare feet.

'What are you doing here?' she asked Alice in amazement.

'I walked with Liza,' said Alice, and walked away, as the mistress who was ringing the bell shouted to Jenny.

It occurred to Alice that she was hardly older than the girls outside the school. She had never concerned herself greatly with her chronological age, even at Melton Balbridge. Until her first pregnancy, she had thought of herself as young. Since then, she had believed herself to be in middle life.

At home, Anatole was in the kitchen. 'I want to talk to you,' he said. Alice sat down. He looked at the great mound of her abdomen. 'Alice, if you care at all about me and our child, you must marry me. And yes, I say it is necessary that it should be legitimate. I was illegitimate. I would never inflict that on anyone else. Be quiet,' he said as she began a familiar argument. 'I know that our child will not suffer from a stepfather who loathes it. I know that being illegitimate will make no difference to its being accepted in our own circle. But I will not have my child suffer for it in the world outside.'

'You mean, if it carries my name it'll be teased about being a bastard?'

'No, I do not. I accept that you want a girl to carry your name. Alice, probably it's only an obsession on my part, but please agree to marry me. I swear to God that I will resign in writing every single right that the law gives me over my wife.'

'You'd better do that,' she replied. 'All right, I will marry you for Finola, on that condition.'

'Finola?'

'That's what I'm going to call her. Finola Adèle.'

'I don't like Adèle. She can be Léonie. And what if it's a boy?'

'Oh, Seamus will do.'

'But you will marry me,' said Anatole.

'I said I would.'

Anatole left the house. Alice picked up the dress she was making. She had done very little work during her pregnancy. She sewed very well, for at Red Lion Square she had earned money by doing the mending ever since she was seven. She sat there for a few moments, examining her conversation with Anatole. She remembered his waking up from nightmares, and whispering and crying to her in the dark. She got up and ran out of the house, and saw Anatole rounding the corner of the square.

'Anatole! Anatole!' she called.

'Alice, don't run for Lord's sake —'

She caught up with him and clasped him in her arms, hugging him so tightly that he gasped. 'I'll be happy to marry you! I'll never let anyone hurt you again. I wish I could see your stepfather burning in hell,' she choked.

'Why should you, and how could you, truly understand what it means to have had a miserable childhood?' Anatole gently loosened Alice's grip and looked up into her sad and angry eyes. 'It is because you have never been successfully bullied that I love you, I think. Come on, let's walk to the tube together.' Anatole paused. He stroked her thin arm softly and looked into her puzzled, flushed face.

'I want to tell you something, my love. I murdered my stepfather. I don't know quite why I've never told anyone before.'

'Mother of God,' whispered Alice, wide-eyed, a few seconds later. 'When? How?' She did not need to ask why.

'You're not horrified, are you?' said Anatole. '. . . *bien que tu sois croyante et pratiquante Catholique* . . .' He was almost sneering.

'Of course I'm not. Of course he deserved it, if a quarter of what you've said is true.'

'Well,' said Anatole, 'as to when I killed him, it was nine years after I ran away, when I was twenty-three.'

'How did you do it, then? Did you shoot him?'

'Oh, no. I wanted it to look like a suicide. I drugged him and his old servant, and then I hung him from a beam. He was quite a weight, you know, it was difficult to get him up there. I left France straight away. I didn't care to go to the guillotine.'

'It's marvellous to have had the courage to do that,' said Alice. 'So he didn't suffer, in that case?'

'No,' said Anatole, 'alas he did not. And it isn't courage, it's having had enough hatred. I wish I'd killed him in a painful way.' His eyes narrowed. 'I wish I'd seen the fear and helplessness in his face that he'd seen so often in mine when I was a child, when he came up on me with that stick.'

CHAPTER 10

***

BRAMHAM GARDENS
EARL'S COURT
April 1917

Finola Léonie Molloy was born in the middle of July 1916 at Aunt Caitlin's house in Oxfordshire, as her parents had intended. Anatole had been worried that Alice would be very unhappy if she did not have a daughter. In the event Alice had refused to feed Finola herself, saying that she had produced the child as she had promised: she had never promised to look after her. Anatole had struggled with bottles for a while as he had when Liza and Jenny had been born, but little Finola was a scrawny, ailing child and ate very little. At length Aunt Caitlin had made him agree to allow her to employ a nurse for the child. The only nurse whom Anatole thought tolerable would not go to London, so in August Alice and Anatole left Finola at King's Norton. Anatole went to see his daughter whenever he could afford it.

Kate walked up and down the platform at Dover station, holding her coat close round her body in an attempt to keep warm. She had waited an hour for the train already. Oh, for the hot fug of the trains which had taken her family, when she was a child, from Edinburgh to Ullapool every summer! Kate remembered the damp banana sandwiches which they had eaten on the train, the itching of her best summer clothes in which she had alway insisted upon travelling, and the brown of the moors in a dry summer, before the heather was in flower.

Kate went into the waiting room, where pre-war posters still advertised excursion trips, and where there was a tiny oil heater. She stood so close to it that she was in danger of burning her clothes, but it did little to warm her. She occupied herself with more warming memories.

Kate was thirty-three. She had been born Kate McQuillan. Her parents, a Scottish father and Jewish mother, had lived in a detached villa in an Edinburgh suburb. They had had one maid and six children, of whom Kate was the youngest. Her parents had believed in the higher education of women, but when Kate had failed to enter university they had suggested that she marry Arthur Jennings. Kate had never known their judgement to be unsound before.

When the train came in, Kate got into an icy-cold smoke-filled carriage. On the way up to London, she found that she could not avoid thinking about Bramham Gardens, about what Anatole had told her in his letters, which had begged her to leave France.

Everyone was up to greet her at Bramham Gardens, though it was two in the morning when she arrived. They had some food ready for her, and Kate ate it gratefully although she was very tired. She noticed that Anatole and Alice did not exchange a single word while she was eating. Alice's face was yellow and drawn. She looked at least thirty. Her hair hung in greasy tails, and her nails were bitten to the quick. Her unwashed clothes stank of smoke.

'Did you hear that Harry refused to do any war-work at all, and they put him in prison?' Jenny was saying as she stood by Kate's shaking elbow. 'That's why Christopher's not here. He's moved into rooms near Pentonville to feel close to Harry. Little advantage that must bring him, though, from one angle.'

'That's enough, Jenny,' sighed Kate.

That night, Anatole slept in her bed for the first time in four years. He did not make love to her.

'Won't Alice have missed you?' asked Kate in the morning, when he was getting dressed.

'I haven't slept with Alice since we came back from Caitlin's,' he replied. 'And I haven't made love to her for longer than that, because I couldn't when she was pregnant. She tired of me the moment I married her, Kate. I have had two wives who have grown to hate the sight of me and have rejected my children. And as well, she is sleeping with Leo Shaffer at the moment — or she was a few weeks ago, anyway. She has found a better lover than me. She actually dared to say so! Do you know she once promised me that she would never let anyone hurt me again?'

'Hate the sight of you, indeed! I never heard such nonsense. Last night she was looking at you like a lost dog, though she's too proud to talk to you, of course, silly little fool.'

'Whatever else she is, she is not a silly little fool, Kate.'

'She was longing for you to forgive and accept her, Anatole, I'll swear she was. I bet she'd have Finola back if you approached her right.'

'I have cajoled and wept and flattered and threatened but it is always no, no, not until she is a year old. The excuse is that the child ought not to be entrusted to our haphazard care till then, because she was so weak at birth.'

'Has it not occurred to you, Anatole, that she might really think that?'

Anatole pulled his shirt down and looked straight at her. 'Do you honestly think it could be that?' he sneered.

'No, I don't. But look, Anatole, a lot of women are very depressed after they've had babies. You men are all the same. You think that you've got a right to abhor the napkins and the yelling but that a mother ought to think her baby's pure joy.'

'Did I ever mind napkins and screaming?' Anatole screamed. 'Did I?'

'No, you didn't. I'll admit. But just because you love children, that doesn't mean Alice has got to, or will.'

'Her own baby, though! She's such a beautiful litle girl now, Kate, you don't know. Just because she was red and wrinkled when she was newborn, Alice said she was a monster.'

'Anatole, pull yourself together. I'm tired and I can't take any more histrionics. Listen to me. One, Alice took absolutely no notice of Michael when he was born, and hardly saw him, so that's what she's used to. Two, it's quite often the mother who needs mothering after she's had a baby. Three, it's you who ought to be looking after her, without even mentioning Finola. At the moment the poor child — and she's only nineteen, Anatole — must feel that you only value her because of her cargo. She's got to be your perfect wife and mother before you'll accept her. But she won't be. She'll only ever be Alice — though Lord knows it's difficult enough to accept Alice for what she is,' Kate added with a sniff.

'There's no need to insult her!'

'Oh, I .see, it's only you who's got a right to reject and criticise her, is it? And how you could criticise her for infidelity I don't know. My god, you and your love affairs have plagued me all these years . . .'

'Oh, be silent! And don't suggest that you haven't had affairs.'

'That's as may be. I'm just telling you at the moment that if you want Alice — and Finola — back, you've got to look after her. And I'm not going to quarrel with you now, Anatole. Please hurry up and leave me alone. I could sleep all day.'

Kate did not go back to France. She went to work in a London hospital. She and Anatole persuaded Alice not to try to paint (for she had produced nothing which she found satisfactory for a long time) but to do some other kind of work, to occupy her and to stop her from brooding. Alice refused to nurse. In the end, Anatole found her a job as a clerk in the War Office through Lady Caroline Fawcett, the mother of one of his pupils; and Alice worked there until the middle of 1919.

When Anatole next raised the issue of Finola, in May, Alice agreed to her return, scarcely voicing her private thought that the child would be better off where there were no zeppelin raids and rations. She took no notice of Finola when she came back, though, and Finola herself hated anyone but Anatole to touch her until she was two and a half years old.

CHAPTER 11

BRAMHAM GARDENS
EARL'S COURT
March 1918

'THE GERMANS ON THE MARNE,' Anatole read in the newspaper. He frowned peacefully, read the first few words and turned over the page.

Upstairs, Finola was screaming.

'Anatole, I can't bear it' moaned Jenny. 'Why don't you go and shut her up?'

'Because I have to leave in three minutes and I shall be late in any case.'

Jenny stared. 'Liza won't go, you know.'

'Liza will go once Finola has screamed enough.'

Firmly he opened the paper at the centre pages and looked at the leading article. He must be imagining that Finola's screams were getting louder. He waited.

Anatole crumpled up the paper and went upstairs. He galloped up the last flight. There was Finola, in her cubbyhole of a nursery next to his bedroom, purple in the face. She was still in her nightdress, sitting on the floor surrounded by bedclothes which she had pulled off the bed. It had been Kate's turn to wake Finola and give her breakfast today, but Kate had forgotten and Finola could not yet walk downstairs: she could only yell. 'Hush, hush, *je te donnerai ton petit-déjeuner*,' said Anatole, scooping up the child, who was tiny for her eighteen months. 'I thought Kate had taken you back upstairs, you see, darling. There, hush.' She let herself relax and be carried downstairs.

Finola could not be left in the kitchen if no one had the time to watch her, for she was at an age when she put everything small enough into her mouth and clambered over everything large enough. In her own room there was nothing to endanger her, so she was sometimes left there for fairly long periods. In the intervals, two or three people at once would play with her, talk to her and cuddle her. There was not enough money to pay a nanny, although shortly after Finola's return it had been decided that she needed one.

Anatole put her in her high chair in the kitchen and started smashing eggs for her breakfast.

'Do you realise that Liza was just upstairs and she didn't even go to see whether there was anything wrong with the child? That bitch Kate didn't feed her,' said Anatole to Jenny.

'I can get her breakfast,' said Jenny. 'You go off. It doesn't matter if I'm late for school; they don't even notice me being late any more, I'm late so often.'

'She's not going to have to eat your scrambled eggs after she's had no food since yesterday, my dear Jenny,' said Anatole, slamming the saucepan down on the stove.

Jenny sighed. 'Anatole, why don't you tell Liza that she's a lazy pig instead of shouting about her to me?'

'What good did telling Liza ever do? She just looks dreamily through you. You know that perfectly well.'

Finola started to whimper. 'Pick her up,' said Anatole. 'I shouldn't be shouting, it upsets her.'

'I suppose she thinks it's her who's made you angry,' said Jenny. 'God, it must be terrible to be a baby. Can't walk, can't talk, can't read, can't even feed themselves or control their bodies at all.'

'Finola is past that stage, thank goodness,' said Anatole, but he was frowning at Jenny and cooking with less vigour than before.

'Yes, but she's still pretty helpless. And she still doesn't talk at all, though she understands everything. Why is it that everyone thinks it's *terrible* when someone is paralysed when they're grown up, and yet we don't think it's awful for a baby to be like that.'

'It is a normal condition which one grows out of, you know,' said Anatole.

'Yes, but it doesn't seem like that to the baby, does it? And that's one's first experience,' mused Jenny, 'everyone being so much bigger than you, so powerful, so strange, and you able to do absolutely nothing. I bet we don't remember being a baby simply because the experience was so ghastly that we've cut it out of our minds.'

'But if you are loved . . .' said Anatole, slowly ladling the eggs on to a plate for Finola while Jenny held the child closely and allowed her to pull her hair.

'That can make things better, obviously. But all the love in the world can't make you able to do things for yourself if you're a baby.'

'So independence is worth more than love ?' said Anatole.

'I think so,' said Jenny, 'certainly in such an extreme case.'

'An extreme case?' said Anatole. 'Jenny, I must go. I shall have to waste money on a bus if I'm to get there within half an hour of the right time. Can you feed her?'

'Of course,' said Jenny. 'It's quicker to walk nowadays, the buses are so irregular.'

'Well, I shall just have to try my luck.'

Anatole borrowed Augustus's overcoat, which was considerably less shabby than his own, and a hat belonging to a cousin of Clementina's who was currently staying at Bramham Gardens.

He took a very crowded bus from Earl's Court to Belgravia, and walked several hundred yards to Eaton Place. The Belgravia streets were quiet. There were no wartime posters on the walls. Well-polished motorcars stood outside the wide white portals of some of the houses. Due influence had preserved even some of the iron railings from requisition.

The door of the Fawcetts' house was opened by an elderly butler.

'I'm afraid, Monsieur Anatole, that Miss Louisa is with Miss Willsford at the moment. It is half-past ten.'

'Then the lesson is cancelled?' said Anatole eagerly.

The butler considered. 'I will inform Miss Willsford of your arrival. Please wait here.' He walked slowly upstairs.

When he at last came back — after Anatole had spent some time on the exceedingly uncomfortable hall chair which had been designated to him — the butler announced that Anatole would be allowed to give Miss Louisa her violin lesson at eleven o'clock. He was meanwhile expected to remain in the hall. Anatole gritted his teeth.

'Psst!' It was Lady Caroline.

'I've been waiting for you for ages,' she whispered. 'Come in here. Whatever held you up so long?'

'A traffic jam,' shrugged Anatole.

'Oh, so irritating.' He did not know to what she was referring.

Caroline was tall and handsome in the manner which had gone out of fashion ten years ago: she was a full-bosomed, dark-haired woman with heavy features and rich colouring. Anatole briefly wondered why he always ended up with tall women when he thought that he was looking for someone nearly as small as himself.

'Tell me,' began Caroline, 'how's your wife getting on in the War Office?'

'It bores her to tears,' he replied, 'but it gives her something to do, which is the important thing.'

'I did think that everyone under twenty-five became a nurse if their parents allowed them to,' said Caroline. 'Your wife is terribly young, isn't she?'

'Yes,' said Anatole.

Caroline came to sit beside him and looked down at the floor.

'Why did you marry her?' she said.

'Caroline, I don't want to talk about it with you, because you can never remember even the commonplace details of my private life, such as my address.'

'Darling! Why are you cross? But you really aren't happy with your wife, are you?'

'I wish you wouldn't refer to Alice as my wife. I always think that Charlotte has been resurrected from the dead when that expression is used.'

'Charlotte?'

'There, you see, you are quite uninterested in my life when it does not affect you directly. I have told you that my first wife was called Charlotte.'

'Anatole, do tell me why you're in such a bad mood.'

'I am not in a bad mood. Could you please tell your damned butler to show me into some room to wait and not leave me in the freezing cold hall.'

'I know, isn't it icy? It's all this economising for the war effort; you see, one feels one must cooperate. Do you know I haven't ordered one new dinner dress this season. Of course, I'll tell Higgins,' she added. 'I'm sure economising can't be a good thing, you know. After all, if one doesn't buy things, trade collapses, and how can that be good for the country?'

'Caroline, you support British trade and industry not when you order twenty-five new evening dresses but when you pay for them.'

'Good heavens, you really are in a bad mood, darling. Whatever's happened? Can't I help?' She put her hand on his thigh. He said nothing, so she caressed him. He pushed her hand away.

'You're tired of me,' she said.

'Caroline,' sighed Anatole.

'Oh, I know,' she said. 'I'm being a tiresome, demanding mistress. What do you want me to be like, Anatole? I've been cheerful and frivolous, and you don't like that, and I've tried to help you and you don't want that either.'

'I'm sorry, Caroline,' said Anatole. He looked out into the street and did not move as she talked.

'You're so lucky, Anatole. Everyone loves and needs you so much. You don't appreciate how marvellous it is to be wanted like that.'

'I know what it is like,' he said.

'Anatole, I don't know what I'd do without you. Since Charles was killed I've been so alone. My husband never sees me any more, and of course it would be worse if I did have to see him. And as for my friends — well, apart from the relief-committee work, of course, one's never even serious with them, let alone intimate.'

'When your sons have been killed, are you serious with one another then?' said Anatole.

'One doesn't say anything except how sorry one is,' said Caroline. 'It's almost as though really showing one's misery is betraying the war effort. It's only with you that I can show myself, so to speak.'

'You must make a new sort of friend, Caroline, and you will have no more need of me,' he said. 'It is bad to depend on one person you know,' he added, for her face, swiftly turned towards him, was trembling, and her eyes were blank with tears. Caroline had always reminded him of someone from his past. Now he remembered that she was a rich, heavy, unhappy, middle-aged woman, very like a lady whom he had known in Paris in 1900. The Parisienne had however not been handsome, but Anatole had then been able to make love to her despite that, as she had been paying him to do. Anatole closed his eyes and wrapped his arms round himself.

'Anatole, please come here tonight.'

'I can't, Caroline, it's my turn to cook and I cannot ask anyone else to do it; they're all working so much harder than I. The other men don't have to cook,' he muttered.

'When will you come?'

He looked at her. He opened his mouth, closed it again and then said, 'I don't know, Caroline. I must go and give Louisa her lesson now. Goodbye.' He went upstairs and waited outside the school room for ten minutes.

Louisa Fawcett, who was twelve years old, managed to look very like her mother without being a turn-of-the-century beauty. A belt was tied beneath her plump waist and her legs were encased in thick wrinkled stockings.

'Monsieur Anatole, the string on my violin's broken,' she said.

'When will it be mended?'

'I don't know, it's so hard to get things done nowadays, Miss Willsford said, with the war and everything.'

'All right, but as I have come all the way here we can have a piano lesson instead. Louisa, don't look so cross, please. I know you hate music, but I can't stop your parents making you learn to play, I'm afraid, and I have to earn my living by teaching you.'

She sat down heavily on the piano stool. 'When I go to school next year I can give up learning the piano. Anyway that's what mother said two weeks ago. I suppose she'll change her mind.'

'Is there any piece which repels you less than the others

which you can play?'

Louisa chose 'Goodbye, Dolly Gray'. Anatole controlled his expression as she thumped out the tune. 'Sing it,' he said, 'if that would help you.' Anatole did not teach her singing and had never heard her voice: she sang far better than she played. He told her so and she blushed.

'Monsieur Anatole,' she said, 'if you don't like teaching, why don't you play the violin yourself? In an orchestra or something?'

'Because I am not good enough,' he said. 'Always remember, Louisa, that I teach because I am an inferior musician. Never respect your teachers.' He said it as though he were angry with her.

Anatole had two hours to wait until he gave his next lesson, which was also in this part of London. He had forgotten to bring any sandwiches with him. Usually, on this empty day of the week, he ate something in the park. In any case it was too early for lunch. Hyde Park would be grey and wet, full of skinny leafless trees. Instead of going there Anatole walked slowly through the red Edwardian streets west of Sloane Street.

To eat in a restaurant near here would cost at least half a crown. He might as well, he thought, spend more than that if he was going to waste his money. He felt hungrier than he had been for a long time.

He found a small restaurant near Basil Street. It was early as yet, but the restaurant was beginning to fill up with people. Anatole reckoned that he must be the oldest person present. The restaurant was filled with small, rickety new tables and chairs. It was not well lit. A very modern gramophone was playing a tango tune in one corner. Sitting at the tables were girls out alone with men who were probably not their brothers; they wore make-up and smoked quite openly and their skirts stopped at mid-calf. If only Caroline's daughter were old enough, Anatole thought, he would have heard a lot about the corrupting effects of the war. Several of the young men at the restaurant were officers on leave and it was at the tables where they sat that the talk and the laughter were loudest.

Anatole ate a small expensive plate of an over-spiced stew

of some kind, and drank half a bottle of wine. It was very hot in the restaurant and he felt almost tipsy though he had drunk so little. He paid his bill and went out to roam around until a quarter to two, when he went to Cadogan Square. He was to see the only pupil of his who had much talent; she performed particularly well, but he scarcely noticed it. Afterwards he went to another appointment in Kensington, and then he returned to Bramham Gardens.

Everyone was out, except for Clementina's cousin Edmund. Clementina had left a note saying she had taken Finola with her.

Edmund Graham had no closer relations than Clementina, who was fifteen years older than he was. He had come to Bramham Gardens to convalesce from a head wound. He was also suffering from shell-shock, but this he sometimes denied. He rarely left his room in the basement and rarely saw anyone but Clementina, but Anatole found him sitting in the kitchen with a half-empty bottle of whisky before him on the table.

'Have a drink?' he said, flourishing the bottle with a gracious expression on his face.

'Certainly,' said Anatole. He poured himself a stiff one.

'Been teaching little girls their scales?' said Edmund.

'Alas, yes,' said Anatole.

'Don't you feel bored, doing that all day?' Or scribbling music or whatever else it is you do. Don't you feel you ought to be out there?'

Anatole looked at him and saw that his eyes were puffy with alcohol.

'Apart from anything else, I would not be considered medically fit for the cannon's mouth,' he said. 'They want strapping specimens of young manhood.'

Edmund waved his hand. 'Totally irrelevant,' he said, 'absolutely irrelevant. And even if that's true — even if that's true — you damned Hun-loving conshies get under my skin. If you want to sit round here in this squalor scratching one another's backs I don't mind that,' he scowled. 'Look at me, you. I've spent three years in the damned trenches and Clementina invites me to this mad household (why on earth don't you have proper servants?)

when I'm invalided out, because she's charitable, is cousin Clem. So I come here and I don't want your damned pity. But all I hear from you is how I've betrayed the human race. You don't even have the damned courtesy to pretend to my face that all that pain was worth it.'

Kate came in. Her shift in the hospital had in theory finished at lunchtime. She threw her hat on the table and fell into the rocking chair by the stove. She took off her stained overall with *Dr McQuillan* sewn on the pocket, and kicked the newspaper aside. One of the cats climbed on her lap as she was pulling the pins out of her hair. She took up a volume of poetry which had been published in 1913. Edmund watched her.

'See?' he said. 'She can go away from the hospital and come back here and forget about everything. You can never ever get away from it when you're out there,' he said. He was shaking.

'I know,' said Kate. 'I spent eighteen months in a hospital in France, if you remember.' She had been dealing with men like him all day and through half the night. She resumed her reading of a pretty country poem which she had found meaningless before the war.

'All right,' said Edmund, 'all right. You know as much about it as a woman can do. But as for you, Anatole — you just sit in your liberal pacifist bath and talk. You're too lazy even to get up and start subverting the war effort which you hate so much. As a matter of fact you don't even talk, not like the rest of them do. You listen to everyone and agree with everyone, you can even understand my point of view. And it's because it all just passes over your head. I don't care if the Germans win now I've done my bit,' he said. 'I just hope the damned war clears away the damned fence you've all been sitting on so that next time you can't sneer at us from up on high.'

Anatole got up and went over to Edmund's chair. He was not quite tall enough to tower over him even though Edmund was seated.

'I've had Kate telling me about the hospitals. I've had Alice telling me about the War Office. I've had Caroline talk to me about her dead son. I've had you talk to me about the trenches. And you all say how lucky I am not to be involved at all, and how I can't possibly understand. If I can't understand, why don't you just leave me alone instead of piling your miseries on top of me?'

'Anatole,' said Alice, who was standing in the kitchen door, 'why don't you ever tell people to leave you alone, in that case?'

'I am telling you!' he shouted. 'And I am going away. I shall go to — to Wales for a month, on my own, and you can take care of Finola.'

He waited for her to look horrified. Kate began to remonstrate. Alice said: 'That's a good idea.'

CHAPTER 12

~

KING'S NORTON
OXFORDSHIRE
Christmas 1919

The house in Bramham Gardens was deserted over Christmas 1919. Kate had gone to stay with her sister in Dundee. Augustus and Clementina had gone to live in a house of their own again shortly after the armistice. Jenny was staying with a friend from her new school, Queen's College, and Anatole, Alice, Liza and Finola had gone to King's Norton.

On 23 December, Liza and Alice were trudging through the woods near Aunt Caitlin's house. They had been gathering holly and they held huge bundles gingerly in their arms.

'I've decided what I'm going to do,' said Liza. 'I'm going to teach myself to type, and then I'm going to try and get a job with a publisher. I'd like to become an editor eventually, and I might be promoted, even if I am a girl.'

'Are you glad you left school in the summer?' asked Alice.

'Oh yes. I didn't feel it was necessary for me to get a formal education, because I can teach myself the things that really interest me just by reading books. It's different for Jenny. You have to have lessons to learn maths and chemistry.'

Soon after she had left school, Liza had got a job as a shop assistant. The hours had been long, the work dull and tiring, and she had been sacked after three months after being caught reading a novel under the counter for the second time.

'You certainly ought to get another job soon, Liza. We need the money to keep Jenny at Queen's,' said Alice gently.

'I know,' said Liza, biting her lip. 'I'm sorry. I will learn to type soon. Clementina showed me how to teach yourself. You have a card with all the keys drawn on in different colours, and you attach the card to the typewriter so that you can't see your hands or the keys underneath.'

'It sounds like creating more difficulties than there need be, to me,' replied Alice.

'Clementina says it's easier.'

'She ought to know, I suppose.'

Liza was nearly fifteen now. She had reached her diminutive adult height, but not her adult width. She looked as though she might, like Alice, retain her adolescent figure throughout her life.

They came across a fallen branch covered with rotten lichen. 'Let's sit down,' said Alice, and she dropped her bundle of holly. Liza joined her, and leaned against the tree trunk, her chilblained hands deep in the pockets of the heavy coat which she had borrowed from Aunt Caitlin.

'I'm sure you could become an editor very soon,' said Alice. 'You've read so much you must be able to tell a fine sentence from a bad one.'

'Oh no, you need training. You think that good prose sinks into you, but it takes years of practice at examining books and writing them to know what makes an effective sentence,' said Liza. 'Sometimes I read my novel and then I look at a really wonderful book, like *Vanity Fair*, and I think about it, but I can't put my finger on what makes my book so turgid compared to that. I cry about it, especially when I think of how well Jenny's doing at her science. She'll probably get a scholarship to Cambridge,' murmured Liza. 'Oh, Kate's so proud of her!'

'Liza, Kate's the first to admit that in a way sciences are less difficult than arts, especially at Jenny's level. Everything just falls into place for her without her thinking properly. There's very little hard work in science compared to literature. One thing's right and the rest is wrong. It's not like that in the arts. It's all much more subtle. I would say that you have to be Newton before you really have to think and use your imagination in science.'

'But don't you see, Alice? Science is just so removed from our understanding, and we're so much less clever than Jenny, that when she juggles those symbols and numbers about it looks to us as though it's no effort for her. It's like watching ballet.'

'I'm glad you're a perfectionist,' said Alice. 'But I wish you didn't couple perfectionism with self-doubt.'

'Don't try to reassure me,' sighed Liza.

They sat in silence for a while. Alice watched Liza's profile, which was pink with cold. Her nose was long and pointed, like Anatole's. Her eyelashes were thick, but so pale that they could only be seen in certain lights. Though the sky was clear today, the descending sun gave out little brilliance. Alice saw it gleaming above Liza's head, casting the shadow of the branches in a net over her frail face. Without thinking, she put out a hand to touch Liza's soft pink ear. Liza jumped, and turned round to face Alice, her lips slightly parted.

'You've got the only colourless face I've ever seen which is interesting to look at,' said Alice. She held out a hand, and Liza took it and drew close to her. Alice slid her arms inside Liza's coat and held her. She laid her cheek against Liza's, which was warmer than she had expected it to be. She kissed it and then, after wondering vaguely for a moment, she kissed Liza's mouth, and found that her lips opened, and that her tongue tasted slightly bitter from the damp black stick which she had been chewing. It was a calm pleasure, not a rush of violent desire such as she might have felt with a man.

Liza put her arms round Alice's neck and then suddenly let go and drew back. She looked at her feet, and held her face in her hands.

'I'm sorry,' said Alice, 'I didn't know I wanted to do that.'

'Oh!' cried Liza. 'It was lovely!' But she looked very worried when she turned again to face Alice.

'Let's get back to the house,' said Alice. 'It's getting dark.'

They picked up their holly again, and continued to tread cautiously through the wood. Liza followed Alice, her eyes wide open, fixed upon her back, and smarting with the cold. Soon they reached the edge of the lawn, and could see the lights shining from the small mullioned windows of the house.

Aunt Caitlin had used to say that even if she found life more comfortable in England, where many of the relations whom she preferred lived, she would go back to Dublin to die. But in view of the terrible troubles in Ireland, she had postponed her return.

It was nearly teatime when Alice and Liza got back. The warmth of the house made them ravenously hungry. They went into the drawing room, where Anatole was sitting with a distant cousin of Alice's, Hugh Tahaney. Finola was on his knee.

'I want to go for a walk,' said Finola.

'Liza, can you take her?' asked Anatole. The colours and smells of the country fascinated Finola, but the lack of streets and people also frightened her, so she would never go outside alone. He gently lifted Finola off his lap.

'It's nearly teatime,' said Alice.

'I want you,' said Finola.

'I'm talking to Hugh, darling.'

'Come on, Finola,' said Liza.

Finola stood still.

'*Il faut accompagner ta sœur, ma petite,*' said Anatole quietly. Finola toddled over to Liza, looking at Anatole over her shoulder.

'Hurry up, Finola,' said Liza. She did not mind going out again: a walk without Alice or Anatole would give her time to think.

Everyone had just sat down to tea when they got back.

All the meals, including breakfast and tea, were enormous at Aunt Caitlin's house, as though the old lady were continually reminding herself that the Great Famine was over. Today there were scones, butter, jam, cream, Indian and China tea, crumpets and two sorts of cake.

Finola nibbled shyly at one thing after another, and tried to stop the food from getting all over her face. She sat propped up on cushions, an enormous napkin tied under her chin, staring round the room. She had spent hours yesterday studying the lacquered Chinese screen in the drawing room.

Anatole sat watching her. She was small for her age, and

she had Diana Molloy's colouring, except for her eyes which were dark grey like his. Alice dressed Finola in odds and ends, as she had dressed herself until she had stopped growing. Anatole thought how much Finola would like his Christmas present to her, which was a proper dress in dark blue viyella.

Finola carefully wiped her hands, and asked to be helped down from her chair. She went over to a small table on which there was a pair of enamelled seventeenth-century scissors. She looked at them without trying to touch.

'Pick them up if you like, Finola,' said Aunt Caitlin. Finola advanced a hand.

'Oh, Caitlin, I don't think that's a good idea,' said Liza, looking at Alice. 'She might break them.'

'Will you please not try and destroy her confidence, Liza,' snapped Anatole.

'Mother of God, Anatole, the child's broken the typewriter and eaten some of my paints in the last month alone,' said Alice. 'And at least they weren't valuable.'

'Alice, can you not see that she has an innate respect for beauty? She even eats tidily in a beautiful room.'

'Tidily?' asked Liza of Alice, nodding her head at the pile of unfinished scones, crumpets and cake on Finola's plate. Alice laughed. Finola burst into tears and ran to Anatole. He took her on his lap. Liza and Alice refused to look at him.

'I think she's marvellously well-behaved,' said Hugh Tahaney brightly. 'When I was her age I was appallingly spoilt. I used to jump on the chairs and take clocks to pieces if I got a chance.'

'It comes of being the only boy for so long,' said Aunt Caitlin. 'How much older were you than poor Robin?'

'Eight years,' said Hugh.

'Young people today think of nothing but their pleasures,' said Aunt Caitlin. 'Dancing and drinking all night, so I hear. And the music they dance to! But perhaps that's being very puritanical. Maybe it's to make up for the youth that was stolen from so many so little older than themselves. But now I come to think of it, this wild dancing and all the rest of it began before the war. Poor Robin,' she said again. 'You always knew which side your bread was buttered, Hugh.'

Hugh winced slightly. 'I was in the Navy before the war started, Aunt Caitlin. But I agree that my luck was stupendous. I never saw a dead man, not once during the whole war.'

'You need not think you were inactive just because you did not end up as cannon fodder,' said Anatole. 'I did absolutely nothing.'

'But my dear chap . . .' said Hugh, and then looked down and started buttering a crumpet.

'Oh, no,' said Anatole, looking hard at him, 'I could have done some sort of useful peaceable work. I ought to have driven an ambulance. I mentioned that to one of my favourite pupils the other day, and she said that my feet would not have reached the pedals. So there we are.'

'The war seems very far away to me,' said Liza. 'I don't have a very good memory anyway, but all I remember about the war is the zeppelin raids, and the girls at school in mourning and . . . the first recruitment posters, too, for some reason.'

'You didn't know anyone who was killed, that's why, and so you lived in a sort of vacuum,' said Alice. 'And you were a little girl during the war, and you're a young woman now. Menarche is a great dividing line.'

Liza flushed slowly. Hugh Tahaney changed the subject. Liza, who was sitting next to Alice, had eaten very little, though she was hungry. She glanced continually at Alice over the rim of her tea cup, and then she would look away and fiddle with her food.

That night, Anatole said to Alice as they were getting ready for bed: 'You know Liza is in love with you, don't you?'

'Oh, I'm sure she's not,' said Alice through her tooth powder.

'She is. She follows you with her eyes. She agrees with everything you say in a bid for approval. Which she gets,' he added. Alice said nothing.

They had been whispering, because Finola was asleep on a small bed in the corner. Anatole turned towards her.

'She'll be four in the summer,' he said after a while. 'Let's have another one.'

'No,' said Alice. 'She's quite enough.'

'Yes, I suppose parenthood comes hard if you're a paedophile,' he hissed. 'You can only love a child in a sexual way, can't you? A child of a particular age.'

Alice slammed the bathroom door on him and locked it.

'Open it!' he cried hoarsely, banging on the door, with one eye on Finola, who rolled over peacefully.

'Don't talk to me about paedophilia, or incest,' Alice called through the door. 'You find Jenny very nubile. Oh, I know you've never touched her. In fact, you haven't touched her at all ever since you started finding her attractive. Well, I prefer Liza.'

Anatole went away from the door and searched for his pipe. He found it, and took a long time to fill and light it, in silence.

Alice slowly opened the bathroom door and came out. Anatole looked sad, not angry or resentful.

'Can't you see, Anatole, that if I did go to bed with Liza, it wouldn't threaten your position at all? she said. 'I only went to bed with Leo to spite you that time. I've never really wanted another man since I met you.' And that's more than you can say, she thought; and dismissed the thought. '*You* can satisfy all that sort of desire. But how on earth can I go to you for the sort of lovemaking I want from a girl?'

'My daughter.'

'Oh, come on, Anatole, you were never very close to her. She's too like Charlotte for that.'

'I am fond of Liza, and I don't want her to be hurt. She's very, very sensitive.'

'I wouldn't hurt her.'

'Oh, Alice.' He shook his head. 'I take your point, and I can't stop you in any case. You have your own peculiar sensitivity, Alice; you know exactly where everyone is vulnerable.' He got up and went to bed. Alice joined him a little later. They did not speak or touch each other.

Liza lay in bed smoking. She was sleeping two doors down the landing from Alice and Anatole. She had heard Alice slam the bathroom door. Her hair was beautifully brushed and lay spread over the pillow. At home, Alice and Anatole had separate rooms, though they usually slept together. Liza heard nothing for two hours after the door was slammed. The next day, Alice avoided looking at her, though Liza followed her silently whenever she could.

Back in London, Liza returned to being Alice's model, her favourite model now. Alice would sometimes touch Liza's pale hair and long wrists and delicate skin. They never went to bed together. Alice said nothing but Anatole guessed that, despite her anger that night, she was not sleeping with Liza.

CHAPTER 13

BRAMHAM GARDENS
EARL'S COURT

October 1922

Clementina had recently bought one of Alice's paintings. Alice took it round to her herself one evening. Finola, who got on well with all the Woods, came with her.

The Woods now lived in Chelsea. Alice intended to walk there, but Finola soon said that she was tired, and that she wanted to take a taxi.

'Mother of God, Fin, we can't spend half a crown on a taxi!' said Alice.

'Oh please. I've never been in one. Just once.'

The painting was quite heavy, so Alice agreed. Inside the cab, Finola pushed herself into the depths of the leather seat, so that she could hardly see out of the thick windows. The taxi was dark and smoky, and she could hear the motor throbbing through the seat. She crossed her hands on her lap and stretched her feet out in front of her.

A year ago, the first time she had ventured out alone, Finola had nearly been run over. Since then, she had never gone out alone again. This had also happened to Alice when she was five, but she had merely learned to cross the street when it was not full of traffic.

Finola pulled herself up, so that she could see the people who were walking, and on buses, and look them in the eye. No one, she found, took any notice of her being in a taxi at last.

Alice stopped the taxi before it reached Clementina's house. Finola complained about this while Alice was paying the driver. 'Don't spoil it by moaning, Fin. It'll be your last taxi ride for a long time.'

'Will you unbutton my smock, please?'

'Whatever for?'

'I don't want to go out in it.'

Alice undid the two buttons at the back of the sleeveless, deep-pocketed smock. It was very like her own, a useful article which Alice had worn since she was very small.

Finola studied the sleeves of her jersey, which were tight and threadbare. 'Can I have a new jersey?' she asked.

'Yes, I suppose so. We can buy one next week. Come on, we'll be late for Clementina.'

Finola trailed behind Alice, who walked very fast. Occasionally Alice stopped to allow Finola to catch up with her. She would frown when she did so, and kick the ground.

Clementina's housemaid opened the door to them. The Woods employed two maids. Finola wondered why they chose to live with such melancholy and silent people as the black-clad maids seemed to be. Of course, they were very polite and helpful, but so much so that they made Finola feel nervous.

Clementina's sitting room was painted duck-egg blue and had a large window at either end. It was furnished with cushioned wicker chairs and an old wooden table, which was scattered with books and magazines ranging from the *Boys' Own Paper* to an illicit copy of *Ulysses*, smuggled over by Augustus from Paris.

'Come on, let's hang it up,' said Clementina, tearing open the brown paper in which the painting was wrapped. Finola went to play with Michael's puppy, underneath the window.

The painting was in oil, and it showed a group of suffragettes in Trafalgar Square in 1913. These suffragettes had been one of the first things Alice had seen on her return from Melton Balbridge. She had depicted the scene in grey, brown, dark blue and indigo, all except for the messages on the suffragette banners, which were in bright green.

'How long ago all that seems!' said Clementina.

'It's rather like a tombstone,' Alice commented. 'I wouldn't really like to have it on my wall.'

'A monument, at least. A little further up at your end, Alice.'

When they had finished hanging it and Clementina stood

back to look at it, Alice caught sight of a copy of *The Interpretation of Dreams* on the table. 'I didn't know you were interested in psychology, Clem.'

'It's Augustus's. I've tried it, and I've never read such pernicious rubbish in all my life.'

'What do you mean? I think there's a lot of truth in the idea that most people's problems are related to their sexuality.'

'That's understating his thesis. Anyway, it's not his theories about sexual repression that I object to. He's so against women, Alice. For heaven's sake, you're partly lesbian yourself. Can you accept some silly little Viennese crank — and a friend of Leo's has met him and said he's never seen such a repressed-looking person — telling you that you have a sexual problem which stems from your having been born without the great mark of maleness? Castration complex, indeed! It's men who've missed out. Wombs ought to mean, and could mean, and perhaps did once mean, power.'

'I can see that he's trying to make a scientific justification for the oppression of women, now that the old methods have begun to fail. But still, don't you think that if his ideas became a sort of public myth, ordinary people would be able to enjoy free love?'

'Perhaps. But it'll take a different kind of theory — and economic system — to create true free love for women. Anyway, I'm not sure that complete free love would be altogether a good thing. Don't attack me, Alice.'

Michael came into the room. 'Hello, Fin,' he said, walking straight over to her without greeting Alice. 'D'you want to come and see my new train?'

'Oh yes, please,' said Finola, surprised. They went out together, with the puppy. Michael led her upstairs.

When Michael was five, and Finola three, and the Woods had been living at Bramham Gardens, Michael had said that he was going to marry Finola. Now Michael had gone to school and, if Finola made any reference to this matter, he brushed it aside. He had not even spoken to her very much recently.

In his room, Michael fished the clockwork train out of his

toy box and put it firmly between them as they crouched on the floor. 'You're my half-sister,' he announced, scowling. 'So you see, even if you do want to marry me when we're grown up, you can't.'

Finola stared at him and he said impatiently: 'Alice is my real mother. Mother told me. So that makes us half-sister and half-brother to each other.'

'But who's your father, then? Isn't it Augustus?'

'No, silly. My real father's dead. He died in the war.'

'But Alice is married to Anatole, so Anatole must be your father.'

'You can have babies before you're married. That's what Alice did. But she didn't want me, so she gave me to Mother.'

'Why didn't she want me — I mean you?' whispered Finola.

'Mother says it was because she was "only sixteen" when she had me. But sixteen's just as grown-up as forty, isn't it? And I asked Mother if other people have babies when they're sixteen, and she said some do, especially poor people, and I said, did they all give them away, and she said, not always. So you do see, don't you? There's something wrong with Alice. She might be mad, Fin. I might have inherited it!'

'She's my mother too,' said Finola. 'She was eighteen when she had me.' She paused. 'But Michael, Clementina and Augustus love you! It doesn't matter to you that Alice didn't want you.'

Michael frowned slightly and wound up the train. The two children watched it go round and round on its track, lying on their stomachs with their heads cupped in their hands.

'But why did she have us?' said Michael.

Finola sucked her thumb. 'I heard Kate say that if only the law would let women stop babies coming, there wouldn't be nearly so many problems around.'

'She means babies are problems?'

'Well yes, I suppose she must.'

Downstairs, Alice was drinking with Augustus, who had just come home. Clementina had gone out for a moment. 'I can't thank you enough for lending me the money, Augustus. I couldn't possibly have asked Aunt Caitlin, she disapproves desperately of abortion, and she can always tell when you're lying.'

'How did it go?' asked Augustus.

'It was agony. The place was clean, though, as far as I could tell. But the worst thing is Anatole. I have a morbid fear that he'll find out somehow and he'd never forgive me. I can't look him in the eye.'

'Yes, he told me he thought there was something wrong with you.'

'It's a terrible thing to live with. I haven't got any excuse, because we've got enough money to have another child, and Anatole and Kate would do a lot of the looking after. We might even be able to afford a nanny this time around.'

'It's your body, Alice. It's quite permissible for you not to want another baby.'

Clementina came back. 'Michael and Fin seem to be enjoying themselves. I do hope this means that Michael's got over this ridiculous girl-hating phase.'

'Oh, that'll last on and off until he's twelve or thirteen,' said Augustus. 'It's the latent sexual phase, you know,' he added, grinning at Clementina.

'I never had this latent sexual phase, and neither did Alice. I remember her pursuing Tom Shaffer when she was nine.'

Tom Shaffer, Leo's son, had been a stretcher bearer in the war, and, having survived, had died of the Spanish influenza in 1918.

CHAPTER 14

KING'S NORTON
OXFORDSHIRE
June 1923

Alice lay on her back in the long grass in the orchard at Aunt Caitlin's. It was early in the month and the depths of the grass were still wet with dew. She shaded her eyes against the sun as it came down through a gap in the leaves made by a sudden gust of wind, and fiddled curiously with a blob of creamy spittle on a stalk of grass. She wrinkled her nose and flicked a worm away.

Finola came running up. She was nearly seven now and was still very small for her age, but she had a thin, serious, delicate face which made her look older than she was.

'Look, Alice, I found twelve different sorts of flowers behind the greenhouse, and I know all their names. You'll catch cold, lying on the grass like that,' she added severely.

Alice laughed. 'Tell me the names of the flowers, then,' she said.

'That's ragged robin, and that's cow-parsley, and that's forget-me-not, and cuckoo-pint, and red campion, and buttercup, and that's a bluebell but it's nearly dead now . . . Alice, why can't we live in the country?'

'Well, we have to work in London, you know.'

'But you could paint and write music anywhere. And Kate could still be a doctor, and Liza could write like she wants to, and, oh, everyone could work in the country,' she said vaguely, as it occurred to her that Jenny could not easily uproot herself from Queen's, where she was just finishing her exams.

'Um,' said Alice, 'but you see, it's not just painting that's the problem. You have to find a market — people to buy things. The market in town's much bigger.'

'Oh,' said Finola.

'But we come here quite often,' said Alice. 'We came in April.'

'Yes,' said Finola.

'I wonder why you're a country child?' said Alice. 'I would have thought that being brought up in London would make you feel that London's the only right place to be, as I feel.'

'But this is different. It's new and exciting,' said Finola.

'I see,' said Alice. 'You don't know or understand anything about it, so you want to know.' She fingered Finola's fine red-blonde hair, which was a more delicate version of Diana's.

'You're an explorer in your way, aren't you? Why don't you want to explore London?' Finola still hated going out alone.

'You couldn't explore London,' said Finola, looking down at Alice in surprise. 'You have to have something new to explore, or you wouldn't be exploring it.'

'That's logic,' said Alice, and grinned. 'Don't look upset, Fin, I wasn't being rude to you. I suppose you're right in a way,' she said lazily. '. . . Fin, if you could plan a perfect life for yourself, what would it be like?'

'I'd live in the country,' began Finola, 'and I'd have lots of brothers and sisters, and I'd have a pet tortoise. I'd sleep in a nursery like the one I slept in when I went to Clementina's at Christmas, with a night-light over my bed. I'd never have to do chores, and I'd have a maid to choose my clothes for me and put them out for me at night to wear next day.'

'Is that how you lived when you were at Clementina's for Christmas?'

'Yes,' said Finola, 'it was the nicest holiday I ever had.'

'Did she make you go to bed at a set time, or anything like that?' said Alice.

'Oh yes,' said Finola. 'She'd tuck me up in bed at half past eight, and then I'd have the light on for a while and read.'

'Why did you like being treated like that?'

'It was so unworrying. Why are you looking cross?'

'I'm not cross. I just think it's odd.' She rolled over on to her stomach. 'Well, Fin, if you want to live on strawberries, sugar and cream, you'll have to marry a rich man, that's all. And I think you'd soon get bored of it.'

'I wouldn't' said Finola.

'Obstinate,' said Alice, and tweaked her hair.

Finola got up and ran back to the old greenhouse. She had left her flowers behind.

The greenhouse was very large. The bricks were decaying and the panes were dim, so that Finola could not see much of the inside. The doors at either end were locked, as they had been last summer. Finola fiddled hopefully with the doors once more and then she walked round the greenhouse, trying to find a loose or open pane of glass. She saw one pane which was tilted forward by half an inch. Banging down the surrounding nettles with a stick, Finola went to the pane and tried to ease it open with her fingers. She stood on tiptoe and one of the nettles bounced up and stung her.

'Here,' said a voice behind her, and she jumped. 'That one's no good. There's a good way in round the other side. I'll show you.'

It was a boy of about nine who was speaking. He wore a crumpled shirt, grey shorts which were too large for him, and a striped belt with a snake clasp. He stalked off and Finola followed him.

'How old are you?' he said.

'Seven,' she replied.

'Coo, as much of a kid as that? See, you want a pen-knife to get these open. Girls can't have a pen-knife, of course; it's not your fault you haven't got one.'

'I've got a pen-knife at home,' said Finola.

'Tomboy, are you?' he said. Finola felt proud, though she did not know why. 'Here, you climb in and push it up from the inside. Want a leg-up? That's the way.'

He gave Finola a vigorous push and she scrambled up over the ledge, grazing her knee quite badly. She quickly squeezed out the tears which came to her eyes, and then she looked around.

It was hot in the greenhouse, with a wet heat which she had never felt before. She was kneeling in a long stone trough full of damp, black, warm earth and on either side of her were tomato plants. Two iron pillars, miniature versions of the painted iron columns on South Kensington station, held up the ridgepole of the roof. Twisted round them was a convolvulus which bore brilliant blue flowers. She gazed at the flowers.

'Here, what's keeping you? Never been in a greenhouse before? Push the window up.'

Hastily she did so and scrambled down from the trough. The floor was covered with red, broken, diamond-shaped tiles. Some of the tiles still had yellow patterns on them.

'The old man's got his peaches through there,' said the boy. He pointed to a door. 'The door'll be locked,' he said, 'but I know how to pick it.'

While he fiddled with the lock, Finola walked round the greenhouse. She found a stone sink at the other end, full of black, stinking water. Gingerly Finola ran her fingertips through the slime on top.

'What are you doing?' he said. 'Look, I've got the door open. I might have taught you how to pick locks if you'd been watching, but I shan't now.'

The second chamber of the greenhouse was even hotter than the first. The peach tree which covered the wall at the end bore a great many leaves and a few small fruits.

'Not really ripe but better than nothing,' said the boy. 'One or two?' he said graciously.

'Oh — oh, just one.' Slowly she fingered the hard, greenish peach.

'You're not from hereabouts, are you?' said the boy. 'What's your name?'

'Finola. I live in London.'

'Oh, a town kid. No wonder you're so green.'

The locked door was flung open.

'*I'll whale the living daylights out of you, boy!*' the second gardener roared. He boxed the boy's ear. Then he turned round. 'And as for you — why, you're Mrs MacNamara's niece, aren't you?' he said, staring.

'Great-great-niece,' she quavered, holding the peach behind her back.

'Well, miss, if you wanted to see the greenhouse you only had to ask me. You don't want to get mixed up with boys like this.'

'Why didn't you say you were from the big house?' said the boy.

Finola looked at him. She thought that he was angry and she said, shaking her head: 'I didn't know that you'd need to know.'

'You get out,' said the gardener to the boy, 'and I'll tell your father on you, make no mistake about it.'

Finola scuttled after the boy and turned sharply round the corner. She went back to the orchard where Alice was still sitting with *Eminent Victorians* open in front of her. Finola considered going to talk to her and decided against it. She wandered slowly round the garden. She felt cold and decided to go back to the house to fetch her jersey and perhaps to stay indoors.

Finola found Anatole playing the harpsichord in the morning room. She waited at the door. If he noticed her she could speak to him, otherwise he would be angry if she interrupted him. He was frowning as he played but not, she thought, with absorption.

'Ah, Fin,' he said. '*Que feras tu aujourd'hui?*'

'*Je sais pas,*' she said, and came over to the harpsichord. 'Are you melancholic?'

'No,' laughed Anatole, 'I am just maddened because Caitlin has had this harpsichord beautifully repainted and has not had it tuned for fifteen years.'

'Anatole, could you explain something?' said Finola. 'Are you busy?'

'I can certainly try to explain something, darling.' He touched her arm. She nearly moved away, as Liza had used to do as a child when he touched her, but then she came closer to him. She told him about the incident in the greenhouse.

'But Anatole, why didn't the gardener clout me when I'd been stealing peaches like he did the boy?'

'He told you, didn't he? Because you were Caitlin's great — however many greats it is — niece and the greenhouse belongs to her and she would certainly let you eat unripe peaches if you wanted to. Though I hope you didn't; it would make you sick. And even if she didn't want you in the greenhouse, the gardener would not hit you himself, he'd hand you over to Alice, I expect. Or to your nanny, if you had one.'

Finola did not say, 'I still don't see why', because a further explanation would take a long time, and because she was thinking.

She went up to her room. It was a small room, painted dark green, and the furniture was very heavy. It was rarely used. Finola had in previous visits shared a room with Liza or Jenny, but neither of them were here now, and she was seven years old and able to sleep on her own in a strange room, she was told, though Aunt Caitlin promised to have the landing light left on. Finola eased herself into the large, slippery chintz armchair and picked up the book of stories which Clementina had given her at Christmas. Her favourite one was 'The Birthday of the Infanta'.

Because this cold room smelled both sweet and musty, like a church, the black and silver church-like gloom of the Court of Spain in the tale did not seem so remote and romantic as it usually did. Finola slowly picked her teeth and read the familiar story.

The Infanta could converse only with children of equal rank, except on her birthday. On her twelfth birthday she was not actually associating with the young nobles who were around her, but then she was twelve instead of seven and probably had not the same need for companionship. Finola had occasionally wondered why the exquisite Infanta was so cruel to the dwarf. She had presumed that it was because he was so ugly and she was so beautiful. She wondered now what would have happened if the Infanta had been friendly to the dwarf, since she could not be friendly to the beautiful noble children because they were a little different. Possibly the Infanta would have liked to have a long talk with the strange new dwarf. Anyone would like to have someone so very infatuated with her as the dwarf was with the Infanta. Finola wondered about the Infanta's name, which was not mentioned. She supposed that to be and to be called Infanta of Spain was enough; her own name would be considered meaningless. Nor did the dwarf have his own name at the Spanish Court.

Altogether the Infanta was a very unpleasant person, but she must have been quite as unhappy as the dwarf if she did exist apart from her clothes, which she surely must do. But perhaps if one had always lived like that one was not unhappy as other people would be. Alice had once said that you cannot want what you have never had.

Finola frowned, and though she had not yet quite finished 'The Birthday of the Infanta' she turned back the pages and started to read 'The Happy Prince'.

Shortly after Anatole, Alice and Finola returned from their holiday, Kate told the household that there was a financial crisis. After supper one evening there was a discussion about economies and alterations to be made.

'We may have to economise,' said Mr Tuskin with a sniff, after various proposals had been put forward and rejected, 'but we simply must have an increase in our own shares. One pound ten a week is simply derisory.'

'Do you realise that most people in this country have to pay for the rent and food and insurance of a whole family on less than that?' said Charlie, a radical journalist who had come to live at Bramham Gardens some months ago.

'Yes, yes, Charlie, but we are members of the upper-middle classes in our own very special way,' said Mr Tuskin.

Charlie breathed in deeply. 'Considering that you and Harry were evicted from your last place for non-payment of rent . . .'

'But my dear Charlie, I thought eviction was one of the greatest capitalist scourges of the working class? Are we to be criticised for our defiant socialist gesture of non-payment?'

'Be quiet,' said Kate. 'I can tell you that our own shares will simply have to be cut, at least until some of us start earning more money. Don't you understand that the rent's been nearly doubled?'

'Some of us,' said Alice, 'just cannot earn a regular income like you.'

'Some of us cannot rely on nice little bonuses from a doting aunt.'

'Oh, go to the devil.'

'Why is it that the discussion of money always brings out

the worst in us?' said Anatole. 'I think there is a lot to be said for the polite view that it is a vulgar and disruptive topic.' He looked quite worried and rather innocent.

'Hear, hear,' said Mr Tuskin.

'Stop trying to change the subject,' said Kate.

'Yes, Madam Chairman,' said Jenny.

'Chair this discussion for five minutes and it'd wipe the smile off your face, Jenny. Liza, will you stop reading that novel and listen? It's your money that's concerned, you know. One thing is certain,' Kate recommenced. 'We can't have a daily woman any longer.'

'That's ridiculous,' said Anatole. 'Are you truly suggesting that relief from difficult cleaning is not worth eight shillings a week?'

'Oh, to save our souls from the indignity of manual labour, what price is not worth paying?' mocked Charlie. 'Yes, Anatole, let's carry on paying Mrs Craddock less than what you'd ever accept for anything, for doing work which you'd never do if there was any way of avoiding it.'

'Oh, Charlie, write that down for your next article but do just be reasonable now,' sighed Alice. 'And I think that, as they never do any housework, the men can all shut up anyway,' she added.

'Surely we can afford at least *one* proper maid?' murmured Liza.

'The theory is quite beside the point,' said Kate, absently stroking Charlie's hand. 'The thing is that we really can't afford it unless we cut down our personal shares quite drastically.'

'Nonsense,' said Mr Tuskin. 'I suggest that we economise on food. I've always heard that the Irish, Miss Molloy, grew to be the strongest peasants in Europe when they lived entirely upon potatoes. Now, if we each ate three baked potatoes a day, and perhaps the occasional piece of cheese and the odd orange . . .' he mused, stroking his little beard.

'Mr Tuskin, you're talking a lot of hot air considering that you can only live on aspirins and strong tea,' said Alice.

'I am trying to improve my own health and morals.'

'Can we please get back to the subject?' said Kate.

Finola was lying on the window seat in the kitchen, with

one of the cats on her stomach. She was sleepily watching the clear darkening sky outside and the people who walked by the window. She could hear them talking as they passed, of clothes, of politics, of India, of school. Slowly she turned her face towards the inside of the kitchen and started to listen.

'I think you're all being silly,' she said after a few minutes. 'You're all really quarrelling about how much money you keep for yourselves, so why don't you just keep all your own money?'

'All right, Fin, how do we pay the rent and the food then?' said Alice.

'Well — if everyone paid a quarter of the money they've got towards all that . . .'

'But then we wouldn't have equal shares.'

'Why should you have equal shares if you don't earn the same?'

'We don't earn the same, but we all work just as hard, that's why,' said Kate.

'But Kate, you've just been telling Christopher and Anatole that they don't do enough work,' said Finola.

'Sharp, aren't you?' muttered Kate. She was too tired to smile.

'And if they don't work as hard as you do,' said Finola, half to herself as she turned back towards the street outside, 'then if they had less money because of it they'd work harder. Yes, that's right,' she said.

'Fin, where did you pick up all these Victorian liberal ideas?' laughed Jenny. 'From Caitlin?'

'I don't care about Victorian liberal,' said Finola. 'I'm talking sense.'

'As a matter of fact she is,' said Alice. Kate looked grateful that Alice had said it.

'I vote against Finola's motion,' said Mr Tuskin.

'Mm,' said Anatole and Liza and Harry.

'Look what she's done,' teased Jenny, 'she's introduced foreign principles and split us up into classes. You're the bourgeoisie, Alice and Kate, defending your property, and the rest of you are the proletariat.'

'I haven't done anything,' said Finola, getting up. Everyone was looking at her suddenly. 'Don't you stare at me as though I'd done something wrong.'

Part 4

BRAMHAM GARDENS
1924–1931

CHAPTER 15

BRAMHAM GARDENS

BRAMHAM GARDENS
EARL'S COURT

June 1924

The guests had all gone. The Green Room at 'Dominique's' nightclub, Soho, was littered with the losses of an evening's dancing. A fan, the feather from a lady's headband, several handkerchiefs and paper flowers, were scattered on the dance floor. Anatole closed the piano and climbed down from the platform. He found a ten-shilling note and an automatic cigarette lighter on one of the small tables round the edge of the room, and pocketed both.

'What's the time?' asked Richard Charteris, who played the saxophone.

'Half past three,' said Anatole. 'Have you rung for a cab?'

'Yes,' said Richard. 'Well, we'll be thrown out any minute now. The old man will be wanting to lock up.'

The Green Room was got up to look like an actor's dressing room. There were weak lightbulbs round the many mirrors, and between the mirrors hung costumes: a panniered eighteenth-century dress, a jester's suit and a lawyer's wig and gown.

'Let's get out,' said Anatole. 'It stinks in here. More people than ever tonight.'

'The numbers will start to drop after Goodwood,' said Richard.

'Is that next month?' Anatole remembered that the fashionable Lady Caroline, with whom he had had an affair during the war, had used to talk about Goodwood.

'Yes, end of July.'

Richard was Kate's lover and fiancé. He was thirty-six

years old. Before the war he had used to lead an acceptable upper-class younger-son's life as an army officer. He had lost a kidney and a foot early in 1915, and he said he was glad of it, because he had then had to leave the army and his father could hardly disapprove. Now he was able to earn money by his hobby, playing the saxophone; and he had an army pension too.

The taxi arrived after they had been waiting outside for a few minutes. They were silent as it sped along Oxford Street.

'What do you think about Alice's new model?' asked Richard.

'She's a beautiful girl at the stage Alice likes best. I don't know any more about her than you do.'

'Neither a child nor a woman,' mused Richard. 'Laura Jones. I really wonder what she was doing in Kensington Gardens at lunchtime on Tuesday. I'm sure she had a school uniform on.'

'She's nervous,' said Anatole. 'Alice has been doing her best to put her at her ease.'

'Alice said she'd ring her parents.'

Anatole opened his mouth to speak but waited until they had swung round Hyde Park Corner. 'We should not talk like this. It's Laura's life, isn't it? She's just trying to earn some money being Alice's model.'

'Don't be ridiculous, Anatole. A kid like that, with a public school accent? In school uniform when she arrived? Alice,' he said, watching Anatole, who was looking very tired, 'is getting very fond of her.'

'She likes people who have been hurt in childhood. She likes to care for them and protect them,' replied Anatole. 'That's the way she expresses her maternal instinct, I've decided. I'm very surprised she isn't more friendly with you.'

'She's got too much to do.'

Anatole laughed. 'I forgot,' he said, 'she's become too friendly with Kate — which is rather odd because they did not get on very well for years. She doesn't like the idea of Kate joining the middle-class morality, marrying you.'

Richard stared. 'But *she's* married to *you*!'

'Oh, that's very different. She was eight months pregnant when we were married, and I insisted on it. We had a proper contract, too, denying me any control over her life. I agree with her,' he said, half to himself. 'We don't even fight much about Finola any more, though Alice worries because she reads children's books instead of encyclopaedias.'

Over the last two months, Richard had imagined and rehearsed the scene in which he would tell his parents that he had married Kate. He was doing so now: they would probe until they discovered that their daughter-in-law was not only thirty-nine but also half Jewish, a divorcée, an ex-suffragette and a practising doctor.

At last he returned to the matter in hand.

'Anatole — this is awfully difficult to say — but don't you mind —'

'That my wife chases after young girls?'

'Well . . .'

'No, I don't any more. I always dreaded her finding another male lover whom she preferred, but since she has discovered her lesbian side she has not taken much notice of other men. And she takes these emotional and aesthetic affairs with girls quite lightly. No, it's not that — it's that this sort of lesbianism is not exclusive, whereas I feel that love for another man might exclude me. So I am accustomed to the situation. Anyway, I find the idea of two attractive women making love quite erotic.'

'So Alice doesn't actually . . .'

'Oh, no,' said Anatole. 'I'm sure not.'

Once they were home, Anatole suddenly did not feel tired. He went into the kitchen and sat down while he boiled the kettle. He shrugged himself out of his tailcoat and undid his white tie, while with the other hand he turned over the pages of Finola's bright school atlas. The map of Europe showed only that which had existed since 1919. Anatole looked, still feeling that this could not be an actual state of affairs, at the small Baltic republics, Poland and the Polish corridor to the sea, swollen Yugoslavia, and the diminutive Austria, Hungary, and Czechoslovakia. Yet, on the other hand, the sprawling old Hapsburg empire seemed to belong to the eighteenth century rather than to 1914.

Next to the atlas there was a sepia drawing of Laura Jones. It was the best Alice had yet done. Laura had an oval face and a creamy skin. There were small freckles under her eyes and over the bridge of her nose. She had almond-shaped green eyes and thick, coarse brown hair. She was not plump, but her figure was smoother and more rounded than the sort to which Alice usually took a fancy. Her heavy pink mouth was crooked: it was tilted up at one end and down at the other, and her lower lip was larger than the upper one. It was a face which Anatole felt ought to be sensuous, and sometimes was, yet in this portrait Alice had caught only the worried look in Laura's eyes, and her odd mouth did not express all that it could.

The next day, Finola walked home from school by the Earl's Court Road route. She paused on her way to look at a sweetshop window. She had just enough money to buy five chocolate mice, or lots of liquorice or mint humbugs, and she decided on the mice. No one stopped her eating sweets, but at home they all so disapproved of them that Finola ate them in the street. Munching, she ambled past Earl's Court tube station. She noticed that there was a new poster up, and gave it a glance. Suddenly she stopped. It was a police notice entitled 'MISSING PERSON'. There was a photograph below, and then some writing:

Miranda Pagett, aged fourteen, disappeared from her Hertford-shire boarding school on Tuesday 5 June. It is thought that she may be in London. Anyone who sees a child resembling her, whether she is alone or accompanied, should inform the police immediately.

The address of the nearest police station was given. The photograph was blurred, but Laura Jones's crooked mouth showed up well.

Finola considered going to the police. Then she remembered the real Laura, and especially her hunted look. 'But oh, this is a real, genuine mystery!' Finola whispered in excitement, and wished that she could tell her schoolfriends without asking Laura's, or Miranda's, consent.

She ran back to Bramham Gardens. She knew that Alice was out painting the portrait of some little boy who lived in South Kensington. Laura slept in Jenny's room, because

Jenny was in Cambridge for the university term. She was not in her room, however, and Finola found her in Alice's studio, sitting in the rocking chair, chewing a biscuit and frowning over a book. She did not seem to be concentrating very well.

'Hello, Laura,' said Finola.

'Hello,' said Laura, surprised. Finola waited for a moment, rhythmically kicking the door. 'Yes?' said Laura.

'Is your real name Miranda Pagett?'

'So I'm wanted by the police already,' said Miranda with her twisted smile.

'Yes, there's a missing-person notice out for you. But none of us will ever, ever tell. Ooh,' said Finola, 'I really feel as though I was hiding in Boscobel Oak with Charles II!'

'Well, you're not,' said Miranda. 'Fugitives really aren't very romantic people. They're too frightened.'

'Oh,' said Finola.

'Please go away, Finola.'

'Oh no, please, I'm dying to hear about how you escaped.'

'It was ridiculously and boringly easy, in the event, so it wouldn't interest you. Go back and fantasise about Boscobel Oak if you want some fun,' sneered Miranda. She walked over to the window. Finola looked round cautiously to see her face.

'I'm sorry if I overheard something I shouldn't have,' said Alice, 'but I could hear you clearly coming up the stairs.'

'It wasn't a private conversation,' said Miranda. 'Finola's found out that I'm a runaway.'

Alice nodded comfortingly. 'But you must know you're safe as houses with us?'

'There's a police notice out for her,' said Finola cheerily.

'Finola, this is not some sort of adventure story! Get out and leave me alone with Alice.'

Finola slammed the door behind her.

'You mustn't take it to heart,' said Alice. 'She's not really all that frivolous. She must just be assured that it's of enormous importance that nobody knows about you. You do want to stay with us, don't you?'

'I'll never go back! I'll kill myself if I'm ever

discovered . . . but I'll have to stay here for eight years, indoors all the time, if my parents are never to find me. You can't endure me that long,' she muttered, pleading.

'Yes I can. Do you want to talk about what made you so miserable?'

Miranda turned round, so that Alice saw only the silhouette of her head against the sky. 'I could never put it into words. Unless you know what it's really like to be born rich and upper class, you'd think I was lying about how terrible it is. Look at Kate — ''Underfed children in Bermondsey due to lack of socialism! People dying of damp and cold in the slums, trying to live on the dole!'' she says. Well, it's all true and all tragic. She wouldn't listen if I told her that the upper class actually pays to keep its children locked in institutions which are always cold and damp, underfed, underclothed, bullied and bored. Why, the children in the slums are getting the best of an English education!' She threw her hands in the air, stood still for a moment, and then crumpled up. She sat on the floor. 'You can't believe me,' she said. 'I'm just a spoilt brat, aren't I?'

'I believe you. I know. I spent eighteen months with an uncle in Dorset, after my mother died. The worst punishment they threatened me with, in their opinion as well as mine, was being sent to boarding school.'

Miranda nodded. 'I don't want to start crying, Alice, so I won't talk about it. Not until my childhood feels really far away. But I want to know whether everyone here will understand.'

'They'll be full of admiration for you. All of them except me are rebelling against their backgrounds in some way. Not Liza and Jenny of course, they were born here. Not Kate either, perhaps. But don't you worry about Kate,' said Alice quickly. 'Richard has taught her that you don't have to be poor to suffer, especially if you're young. It took Richard to do it, though, I'll admit.' Alice sighed. 'Sometimes I think it's considered a crime and a madness to be a child.'

'Not according to British justice, Alice,' said Miranda sweetly. 'You don't have to have a trial before you're put in a boarding school or an orphanage. In pointing out the invalidity of Habeas Corpus in this case, I'm acting,

114

dramatising, lying, and trying to get attention, you know. Ask anyone who knows about children.' She burst out laughing.

'I wish you weren't so sophisticated, Miranda,' said Alice. 'You've no need to be any more.'

CHAPTER 16

BRAMHAM GARDENS
EARL'S COURT
January 1925

Finola was going out to have tea at Julia Morton's house. She had put on her neatest, most Julia-ish skirt and jersey that morning, and plaited her hair too. Julia lived in Baron's Court Road. The two girls walked there after school, by which time it was already nearly dark.

Mrs Burton opened the door to them. 'So this is your friend, Julia. What's your name, dear?'

'Finola Molloy.'

'Oh — well, you two girls will want to have your little tea alone, I expect. Julia, I've laid it up for you in the front room. Mind you clear it up when you've finished.'

Julia smiled delightedly. 'Thank you, mum. Is Eddy back from school yet?' she asked. Eddy was her small brother.

'I've just sent Linda to fetch him. He'll be wanting to play in the front room when he comes back, but just this once you can tell him he's not to, as you've got — Finola.' She smiled briefly at Finola.

The two girls went into the front room, in which there were two dim, shaded electric lights, a horsehair sofa, a mirror shaped like a fan, a dark patterned carpet, and a little table, set in the middle of the carpet. The table was covered with a lace cloth and had two plates and two cups with saucers on it. There were small forks, of a sort which Finola had never seen before, beside the plates, together with little spoons and knives.

'Isn't it ever so nice here? I feel just like a grown-up lady. Dad bought that lovely clock just after the war, when trade was doing well,' said Julia, grown-uply, pointing at the clock.

'I've never seen a room like it,' said Finola.

'You're so lucky not to have a brother,' sighed Julia. 'They do make such a noise, and they're allowed to. Well, more than girls are, of course.'

Mrs Morton came in with a tray, on which there were boiled eggs in special cups, sandwiches and a cake. Julia had persuaded her mother that, because Finola was half French, it was necessary to impress her with the elegance of their lifestyle. Mrs Morton had noticed that Finola wore boys' socks and boots instead of white socks and shoes. She stayed in the room when the girls began eating, and saw that Finola was pushing in the top of her boiled egg with her thumb.

'Is your mother French, dear?' she asked Finola.

'No, she's Irish, my father's French.' There was a brief silence, a puzzled one on Julia's side. Finola looked at Mrs Morton. 'Oh, I'm not a bastard, my parents are married but Alice kept her name and gave it to me. If she had a boy he'd take my father's name, but she says she won't have any more children.'

Mrs Morton blinked. The other day, she was quite certain she had heard Julia, in the bathroom, say 'bugger'.

'What's your father's job, dear?' She sat down. She no longer thought it important that the little girls be left alone together to chat.

'He's a musician. He plays the piano in a nightclub, and he composes, too. My mother's an artist.'

Julia suddenly asked: 'What did he do in the war, Fin?'

Finola pushed a crust of bread into her egg. 'He wasn't able to fight, he's too small.'

'Did he work in munitions, then?' asked Mrs Morton. 'Or perhaps an office job?'

'No, he didn't do anything to help kill people. He carried on giving music lessons. After all, you need ordinary people in a war, don't you, as well as soldiers? But Alice — my mother — she worked at the War Office at the end of the war. Kate was a doctor in St Thomas's hospital, but she was in France for a time too.'

'Who's Kate, dear?'

'She lives with us. She used to be sort of married to Anatole — my father — I mean she lived with him for years — but now she's going to marry someone else.'

Julia was beginning to think that her mother was being nosey, and she sat silently eating. Mrs Morton said brightly to Finola: 'Have you any brothers and sisters?'

'Two sisters. They're nineteen — twins. Jenny's reading chemistry at Cambridge and Liza works in publishing. They're my father's daughters by his first marriage.'

'Dear me, well, I shouldn't be interrupting your little tea-party, girls. I'll go now. Julia, when Finola's gone, you must do your homework before bedtime.' Bedtime was at half past seven for Julia. It was five already. Mrs Morton left and the girls helped themselves to bread and butter.

Julia took off her spectacles. She had pretty blue eyes. 'Are you going to carry on at school after fourteen?' she asked.

'I don't know. Alice wants me to leave school, because she says the education is bad. Well, she says it was pretty bad at Cressida Lake, where Liza and Jenny went. She wants to give me lessons at home but I'd rather be at school.'

'I'm going to Kilbride Private School for Girls when Dad gets promoted,' said Julia. 'They wear red hats and proper gymslips there.'

'Is it a day school?' asked Finola.

'Yes,' sighed Julia. 'Oh, wouldn't you like to go to boarding school?'

Julia had lent Finola several school story books by Angela Brazil. Finola rubbed her nose and thought of Miranda. A sturdy glamour clung, for Julia and Finola, to the country boarding schools in books. From them they heard of match teas, dorm feasts, house colours and cosy yet lofty seniors' studies. These things which they had never seen or done were described in detail in school stories and comics, but casually, as though everyone really knew all about them. Julia really felt that she did know all about boarding school. Finola did not, because of Miranda's description of it.

Finola and Julia discussed school, other girls, the hateful-ness of boys, and hopscotch. Julia showed Finola her doll, who had real hair and rolling eyes, and who wore a fashionable dress of pink silk with a low waist. Julia had made a string of long beads for her neck, and told Finola that it had taken her an hour to thread them, and that the beads had cost sixpence. Julia got threepence a week pocket-money. She knew that Finola's parents were too poor to give her pocket-money. She hoped that her mother would excuse Finola's table manners because of this.

Mrs Morton came in again. 'You must practise your new piano piece, Julia,' she said. She smiled at Finola, who grinned back — cheekily, Mrs Morton thought. Finola saw a book which was on a shelf near the door.

'Oh, Julia, can I borrow this? I haven't read it.'

'Oh, yes, if you like. There are some ever such good stories in it, except there's a long one in the middle about love.'

It was a thick, blue book, with a girl's sweet face on the front, called the *The British Girls' Annual*.

'Well, I'll see you tomorrow, Jules. Goodbye, Mrs Morton.' Finola flattered herself about her politeness. She did not, Mrs Morton noticed, say, 'Thank you very much for the lovely tea.'

Finola put on her coat, which was an old jacket of Anatole's with the sleeves rolled up. On the way home she remembered what Alice had told her about being diplomatic about oneself with people who lived in a different way. Mrs Morton had wanted to know quite a lot about Finola. Perhaps one ought to have said that Anatole played in an orchestra. Mrs Morton did not look as though she would fit into the nightclub which Anatole had described.

To be polite, Finola would have to ask Julia back. No doubt she could rig up a lace-covered tablecloth in the cold drawing room at Bramham Gardens, which was only ever used for entertaining the odd stranger, and guide Julia past the kitchen. The only thing Finola had been told about courtesy was that you ought to make people feel at home in your house.

Finola wondered what the little forks had been for. She ought to have them, for ornament presumably, when Julia came. Julia had, in the middle of conversation, eaten her cake with her fingers like Finola.

'Hello, where've you been?' asked Alice from the kitchen as Finola came in.

'Oh, having tea with Julia Morton.' Finola was usually home by five. She went over to the stove and sniffed. 'Ugh, not that beetroot soup again.'

'Have cocoa if you want,' said Alice. She glanced at the title of Finola's new book. 'Did Julia lend you that?'

'Yes.' Finola felt Alice's contempt on her shoulders as she hunched them and sat down to read the book.

'Do you really find that book interesting?'

'Yes. It's fun.' Finola twitched over a page. 'I do like it! It's about nice, ordinary people who can be — jolly! They don't have people wanting them to be interested in things like art and politics!'

'Our life is very ordinary,' said Alice. 'We just try to live with the minimum of fuss and convention in a world which is full of unnatural and cruel social pressures of the kind which Miranda ran away from,' Alice lectured.

'What is the book?' asked Miranda.

'*The British Girls' Annual* of 1920,' said Alice.

'All about ordinary middle-class people happily conforming to their safe little savage world, yes.'

'You're as bad as Alice! You're worse!' screamed Finola. 'You're so like her it's not true. You even talk with her accent, only hers is faint and yours is much stronger, because you want to be just like her, and you're as bad an intellectual snob and as fanatical a hater of ordinary people, so much so that you'd neither of you ever dream of talking to someone who's clean and tidy and has a maid . . .'

'Clementina's very tidy, and she has two maids and a cook,' Alice pointed out. But she looked crestfallen. Finola stormed out with her *Annual*.

'She's right,' said Alice. 'We were awful about it. I'll never comment on what she does again.'

'Oh, Alice, don't talk nonsense. Anyone would think you'd tried to confiscate the book. All you did was make it clear that she's reading rubbish.'

Jenny had been reading and listening in the corner. 'You know,' she said, and Alice looked surprised to see her, 'it's a bad idea to send Finola to the Council school if you want her to pick up proletarian attitudes, or liberal ones. All the kids who go to that school live in Baron's Court, places like that. They're all petit-bourgeois, frightened, competitive and conservative. Finola's drinking in the spirit of the lace curtains and the aspidistras, and she's certainly learning nothing. If she wants to go to school, why don't you send her to Cressida Lake?'

'We can't afford it, that's why. When Kate and Richard go off and get married there'll only be three of us earning in the house. We've got to get some more people somehow.'

'Don't tell me Caitlin hasn't been bullying you to let her pay for Finola's education!'

'She has, yes. Actually, I did suggest it to Fin, but she said she was quite happy at the Council school. And she won't consider letting us teach her.'

'She wants friends of her own age. How's she going to meet them if she doesn't go to school?'

'What do you mean, she wants friends of her own age?' asked Miranda. 'Nine-year-old girls are utterly vile, stupid little bullies on the whole, or else scared nincompoops. It's not their fault, it's their training, but they are. It's absolutely impossible to have friends of one's own age if one's got any brains.'

'Let's admit that Fin's not very brainy,' said Alice.

'Of course she's got brains!' said Jenny. 'Anyway, I think you should persuade her to go to Cressida Lake. Lots of the girls there go to Queen's or St Paul's or North London Collegiate afterwards. Fin certainly ought to learn something if she goes there. And the fact that the girls have money makes them less snobbish, not more so. I mean, girls of that class are not the market for that ghastly book Fin's got at the moment.'

'All right, I'll have another go at her. But Anatole feels badly about letting Aunt Caitlin pay.'

'You and Miranda could persuade him. Well, I must go and do some proper work.' Jenny left.

'It sounds odd, hearing her talk about work. All the time she was at school she messed around,' said Alice. 'She always did well, though, unlike poor Liza.'

'Why did you find Liza attractive?' said Miranda

suddenly, her chin poised on her smooth white hand.

'I don't any more. But she had such charm at fourteen, you don't know. Just like a snowdrop. She still looks her best in January and February, don't you think?'

'She's so colourless.'

'It can be enchanting.'

Miranda stroked her own delicately coloured cheek. She was the best dressed person in the house, and took great care of her appearance. 'Don't look like that, Miranda. You know very well that all other girls are ugly compared to you.'

'But you like ugly people. Look at Anatole!'

'That's different. He's a man.'

Their conversation was interrupted by the entrance of Liza. Liza was smaller than Jenny. She now wore her thin blonde hair in a bun, like Miranda, and for work she wore tidy print dresses. Her face had become very thin. She had brought a friend with her.

'This is Volodya,' she said, putting a pile of papers on the table. 'He needs lodgings, so I thought perhaps he could move in when Richard and Kate go.'

Alice looked him up and down. He was tall, brown-haired, scruffy-looking, with a short, small, curved nose. He was aged about thirty. 'Of course you can if you like. From April, did Liza tell you? We share all our money here.'

'I've warned him,' said Liza. 'He was in favour of Kerensky, you know; he only got out of Russia to save his life,' she added.

'Oh, I hope you can tell us something about what really happened,' said Miranda. 'We only get information through the capitalist press.'

Volodya laughed nervously, and stood twisting his hat in his hands.

'Sit down and have a drink,' said Alice. 'Whisky, gin or beer?'

'Gin, please,' he said. 'I think your system of dividing the income is most just.'

'Good,' said Alice. 'You're staying for dinner, aren't you? There's enough to feed an army,' she said, stirring the soup.

'Yes, Liza invited me,' he said, looking at Liza.

Leo, Clementina, Michael and Mr Tuskin were also coming to dinner.

All thirteen people sat packed round the long deal table in the kitchen. Alice, looking at the faces of those around her, wondered for the first time at how much they had aged since she had first met them. Clementina and Leo were both grey-haired, and Clementina's spectacles were now so thick that her eyes could hardly be seen behind them. Leo's massive figure had sagged and spread, so that he was now enormously fat. Even just after the war, he had looked very young for his age. Michael Wood was ten, and Alice suddenly saw in him a resemblance to Luke. Perhaps it was the way in which his hair curled over his forehead. My son, she said to herself. She felt nothing. Anatole had aged considerably in the last few years. His pale skin was still smooth, but when he laughed his face became riddled with tiny lines. His hair was entirely grey at the front, and still dark in a long stripe down the back. Kate, too, was in her forties, and looked it. She dyed her hair to keep it black, and her blue eyes were now folded into her face by swarthy skin. Of all the adults at the table, only Mr Tuskin looked exactly as he had done in 1904, when he had first begun to teach Alice. Alice herself was nearing thirty, but she had changed little in comparison with the others.

The house had aged with its inhabitants. It had not been redecorated since 1912, and the paint on the kitchen walls was chipped and peeling. The kitchen had once been the dining room: it would have looked very proletarian, with its laundry steaming over the crowded table, had it not been for the elaborate carved cornices.

'Leo, you carry on as though nationalisation would end all the miners' problems,' Alice interrupted when she started to listen to the conversation again. 'I can't for the life of me see how you can improve conditions by replacing several capitalists by a huge bureaucratic state.'

'Do you suggest then that you leave the mine owners alone? Let them scrape up a few more pounds by allowing them to leave insecure pit props, and put hundreds of men at risk?'

'Of course I don't. I suggest that the miners own and

manage the mines. If they dig the coal out, the coal belongs to them by right. And ownership by the miners isn't the same thing as nationalisation, whatever Fabians say. The State isn't the same as the people, and never can be.'

'Indeed it cannot,' said Volodya.

'It might be if it were sufficiently decentralised,' said Clementina. 'But honestly, I can't see how cooperative ownership of the mines, if it could work, could bring the miners a decent wage, in the present economic crisis. Do we agree that the miners ought to get at least £8 a week? Good. Well, the only way they'll get it is if the government pays them that out of public money.'

'But the Tories aren't going to do that,' said Alice.

'No more will Ramsay Macdonald, for that matter,' said Kate.

'Well,' said Leo, 'let's hear the mine owner's case. Come on, Miranda, you can be Devil's Advocate. What would your father say?'

'Oh, of course, he thinks privately that any form of barbarity which increases his income is a Good Thing,' said Miranda, 'but he wouldn't say so. Actually, I'm not sure quite what argument he would use to justify his position. Naturally, I never knew him as a person.' She helped herself to more macaroni. Her face took on a shut look. She only talked about her family to Alice.

Leo turned away from her. Miranda listened, half-smiling, to Finola's eager questioning of Volodya. He was very indulgent.

'So what did the Reds do with your family jewels?'

'Oh, I expect they sold them and used the money for some Bolshevik purpose.'

'Didn't you escape with anything?'

'One sapphire, which I hid in the heel of my boot, and a hundred and twelve roubles,' he smiled. He was making it up about the sapphire.

'Did you used to be a prince?' said Finola.

'No, no,' he laughed. 'Only a little provincial landowner. Most of my land was mortgaged anyway.'

'Oh, but you're still romantic!'

'You're incorrigible, Finola,' said Miranda.

124

'Where did you go when you escaped?' continued Fin.

Miranda gazed up at the rails of airing clothes and sheets which were suspended by ropes and pulleys over the kitchen table. The rooms in this large, dilapidated, rusty brick house formed, she felt, her first real home; and yet it too was an enclosed world. She met only everyone's oldest friends. Liza had given her many assurances about Volodya yesterday. She had only gone out of the house a few times since November, when she had first ventured outside. Here, she could always be alone if she liked. If anyone was occasionally hostile to her, Alice was always at her side. Naturally, Bramham Gardens was no more like boarding school than it was like the mansion in which she had been brought up.

Miranda felt dizzy from drinking too much gin. She excused herself, and left the table. She climbed the stairs to her small room on the second floor. It was bare, except for a bed, a table, a chair, some books and her clothes. It was cold in the room, and she put the eiderdown round her shoulders. She went over to the window. She saw a taxi drive up to a nearby house, and a man in a bowler hat, who was carrying the evening paper, got out. Oddly enough, things from the outside, like delivery vans and bowler hats and the *Daily Telegraph*, surprised her when she saw them from this house, just as they had made her feel cold and strange when she had seen them within the grounds of her boarding school.

CHAPTER 17

BRAMHAM GARDENS
EARL'S COURT
October 1925

Alice stood at her easel, scowling, with a cigarette hanging from her lip, her hair strained back out of her way. Anatole sat under one of the windows, obstructing the light which fell on Miranda as little as possible. He hummed to himself and very occasionally scribbled on the music paper before him.

Miranda was posing nude on Alice's bed. Light fell on her from in front and from behind. She looked sleek and utterly contented. In the painting, Alice had made the room darker than it was, so that Miranda's body seemed irradiated. Alice had already completed one picture of Miranda naked. That one showed only hints of her body and face: round white curves on which the light happened to fall in varying degrees of strength, only hinting at the remainder.

'Do you remember the young beech trees at Caitlin's, the summer Finola was born?' asked Anatole suddenly. 'In the evening? Miranda, if you were a tree, you would be one of those.'

'Really, Anatole, you ought to take up poetry,' Miranda replied with an exquisite smile.

'Keep still!' snapped Alice.

There was a knock on the door. 'Who is it?' Alice called, surprised at the knock.

'Me,' replied Mr Tuskin.

'Wait a moment,' she said. 'Miranda, put the blanket over you.'

'I'm not embarrassed,' cried Miranda.

'No, Mirandolina, but he would be, remember?'

Mr Tuskin put his head round the door and then came in. 'Miss Molloy, why was I not told that you were going to have an exhibition of your own? I only found out from Leo yesterday, yet I hear that the plan was in the offing weeks ago!'

'I forgot to tell you. I suppose you want to choose the exhibits.'

'Naturally,' he replied, raising one eyebrow at her.

Alice laughed. 'It's thirteen years since you were responsible for my work.'

'Nonsense, Miss Molloy, there is still a great deal for me to criticise.'

'Yes, but Christopher, you have criticisms to make of Vermeer and Watteau,' said Miranda coldly. 'And you've never had any of your work exhibited.'

'Don't be impertinent,' said Mr Tuskin, without irritation.

'You don't need to worry, Miranda, I can defend myself.'

Mr Tuskin walked over to the easel and studied the portrait of Miranda from different angles. 'I once set out to paint the portrait of the most beautiful boy,' he commented, 'but alas, he came from such a respectable family that I was unable even to persuade him to take off his clothes.'

'How's Harry?' said Anatole.

'I'm afraid that he's never quite recovered from having been in prison,' said Mr Tuskin. 'The food they gave him there was most harmful to the digestive tract. Twice-cooked meat is so constipating. But apart from that, he's quite well. Now, Miss Molloy, are you going to show me the work you and Leo have so far decided on?'

Alice fetched the stack of five oil paintings which were leaning against the wall, and a portfolio of drawings and watercolours.

Mr Tuskin examined everything, twitching his lip, wrinkling his nose, and screwing up one eye and then the other. Four of the oil paintings were of London scenes, and the fifth was a portrait of the Bramham Gardens cats, who were called Melbourne, Palmerston, Gladstone and Disraeli. Their names were the picture's title.

'If you ever do become renowned as an artist, Miss Molloy

— creditably renowned, that is, not as a portrait-painter — it will be as a painter of London,' said Mr Tuskin. He was holding a painting entitled *A Child's View of Ludgate Hill, 1903*. Alice's jaw dropped.

'Are you all right, Christopher?' teased Miranda. He ignored her. One's first impression of the painting was that the street and the people had been deformed by the artist, but on looking closer it became clear that this was because it was painted from a five-year-old's level of vision. Some subjects were painted as a large muddle, others, such as the City man who was poised in the bottom left-hand corner looking down disapprovingly on the invisible child, were very observantly depicted.

'I suppose the one of the Round Pond is charming,' said Mr Tuskin, 'but a little tedious. Nothing in it surprises one. I don't think it should be included.'

'Alice, can we finish for today?' asked Miranda, as Alice began to argue with Mr Tuskin.

'Oh, of course, if you're tired.'

Miranda went downstairs to get dressed. She came back again with her hair still loose, and asked Anatole to put it up for her. He gladly deserted his pretence of work to do so. She sat in front of him, listening to Alice's conversation and commenting on the paintings. Anatole slowly twisted the coarse, shining strands of her hair round his hands, pulling it back over her soft ears. He touched one of them gently, and stroked its curve, but Miranda only fidgeted as though a fly had settled there.

Suddenly she noticed that she had not got her watch on. 'Where's my watch?' she said, biting her lip.

She went over to the bed, and searched amongst the covers and on the small table beside it. 'Oh my God,' she whispered. 'It's absolutely vanished! It can't possibly be anywhere but here.'

'It might be in your room,' said Alice. She never knew what to do when Miranda lost something. She was no good at searching, and Miranda was never calm until the object had been retrieved. To shout at her for being silly, as Kate had done, made her worse. Alice picked up the portfolio and took Mr Tuskin off to have a drink and look at the drawings in the kitchen.

'It can't possibly be in my room, it really can't be. I remember putting it here, here, next to this book! Oh God, why do these terrible things happen to me! Why must they do this to me? What shall I do if I never find it? Why is life such hell? I'll never, ever find it!' She was crying, and her eyes were red and wild with fear. The watch she had lost was valuable and handsome, a present from a godfather of whom she had been fond; but she had been as upset over the loss of her hairbrush.

Anatole, who had been watching helplessly, suddenly got up and shook her, and slapped her face to calm her. 'Sit down, Miranda. Come on.' He took her over to the bed. 'No one is going to punish you for losing something. No one is going to steal your things because they want to see you punished. That's what the others did to you at school, didn't they? That's why you are like this?' He was sitting on something hard, and, putting his hand in the pillow case, found the watch and put it round Miranda's quiet wrist. 'It happened to me too,' he said. 'I made myself forget, but my half-brother did it to me. I know that, in childhood, the consequences of losing anything are terrible.'

Miranda started to cry again, but in a different way. 'Do you know what it's called?' she said. 'It's called "teaching you to have a sense of humour".'

'Teaching you to be passive under continual humiliation,' said Anatole.

'Exactly. "Oh, Miranda, you must learn to take teasing," they say. How can it be just to laugh at or tease someone who doesn't understand and can't hit back? And, of course, there's never anything funny to laugh at.'

'All humour is cruel,' said Anatole, stroking her hair. 'It always consists of laughing at the misfortunes of others.'

'They used to hide my games clothes,' sobbed Miranda, 'because that was the worst. Once my lacrosse stick was gone for three days. The games teacher made me write a thousand lines saying, "I must not be careless." "You mustn't be careless, Miranda," the girl who'd hid it said to me when she handed it back. I hit her with it and knocked her out. Then they put me in solitary confinement for a week. That, of course, was my happiest week at Radfield. They fed me on bread and cheese as part of the punishment, but how delicious that was in comparison to the school food. They used to force us — I *mean* force — to eat scrag-end of neck, cod, brains, tapioca and junket.'

Anatole shuddered. 'Weren't you all ill on that?'

'Certainly we were. Every February there was an influenza epidemic, and every girl went down with it because they put the sick girls in the dormitories with the healthy ones. I didn't find that so bad as constipation, though. I honestly thought that I would die, my first term. I begged and begged for some syrup of figs. "Don't be ridiculous, child, you're just not trying," said the matron.'

'How long were you there, Miranda?'

'Five and a half terms. I was twelve when I went. I'd had a governess till then.'

'Was that better?' Anatole had never heard details about Miranda's childhood before; for she had never told him, and Alice regarded them as confidential.

'Well, she was dull and cruel through lack of imagination like most people are, but of course it was better, because there weren't any other girls. Before her, though, I had a very nice governess, but she left, I don't know why, when I was nine. I suspect that my father sacked her because I didn't know the Kings of England and my twelve-times table. Teaching that sort of thing wasn't Miss Heaney's method.'

Miranda closed her eyes and let her taut body sag for a moment. 'Oh well, this is all quite irrelevant,' she said a little later. 'It's over, like you said.'

'It's not over, Mirandolina,' said Anatole, 'not while you're still suffering so much from it.'

'Only because I let myself. Pure self-pity.' Miranda made her upper lip stiff.

'You must have been told that for a great many years,' said Anatole. 'Everyone comes to believe that sort of thing, once their own sufferings are in a sense "over". That's why children go on being cruelly treated from generation to generation.'

'Some people believe the lies they're told about themselves

— and about other things, but chiefly about themselves — even when they're still children. Most do, as a matter of fact.' Miranda paused. 'I'll never forgive myself for believing what they told me for two terms — my third and fourth terms. I was quite a rebel when I first went to school, although I didn't actually break a single rule. But the mistresses and the other girls could tell that I hated and despised them — that frightened them much more than disobedience. That's why they told me I was mad, perverted, corrupt, loathsome.'

'Perhaps a child who is an unbeliever is a disease in the body politic,' said Anatole. He lit his pipe and watched her. Miranda was very white. She had vomited out her emotions and she felt very reasonable.

'I've been very crude, you know,' she said, as she slowly wound up her wrist watch. 'I used to think that the authorities — you know, just hated disobedience itself. But in fact, actual obedience rather frightens parents and schools — they think it's unnatural for one not to actually break rules. What they really want is a sort of passive obedience: they don't mind if you break the rules, so long as you accept the punishments they mete out in absolute submission as completely just. I must go and think it all out properly.'

She paused.

'No,' she said, 'I'll never forgive myself for giving in that time. I remember being thrilled when I heard some senior saying "that young Pagett's coming on quite nicely" — meaning that I'd started to really conform. My God! The terrifying thing is that it was so very easy to give in, and the rewards were so great. I was hardly bullied at all those two terms. And I had two friends.'

'Don't be so hard on yourself,' said Anatole, 'it's very understandable that you should have left off struggling after seven years. And remember, you must have been in a great state at that age, just coming up to your menarche.'

'It was my own fault that I was so unhappy. No, I'm not just being conventional. I mean that if I'd either understood none of the truth about my position, or all of it, I'd have been better off. But I just had a very little knowledge; I could see half-way through them all but not the whole way. I'm just not quite clever enough!'

'What nonsense,' said Anatole. 'Do you think that at the age of six you should have intellectualised all your pain as you're doing now?'

Anatole put his arm round her waist. She sat there, looking into his eyes. He drew her head towards him and tried to kiss her but she shook herself away.

'No,' she said.

'Why not?'

'Because I don't want to, that's why.'

'Is it because of Alice?'

'I don't know. No, it's not that, I simply don't find you attractive.' She saw, looking at him, that he had never been in this position before, and she laughed.

Then she said: 'It's very odd, you know, talking to someone who really does understand. Rather frightening, in fact. I was right not to talk to you all that time — now you have a sort of possession of my mind. Alice doesn't. She understands — in the sense that she's happy, and it angers and upsets and puzzles her when someone is not happy — but she doesn't know.'

She went out, and left Anatole staring after her.

—◄—

CHAPTER 18

BOND STREET
MAYFAIR
February 1926

Alice and Miranda were in the West End having tea in Lyon's. They had just been buying material to make new curtains for the kitchen and had also bought various things which they had not intended to buy. They were sitting at a table by the window with their parcels at their feet. Miranda was dressed in black. She wore a hat which was more broad-brimmed than was fashionable, from which there hung a veil. She had discovered that mourning clothes, like an injury, caused people to look away from her.

Through the thick veil Alice could still see, as she gazed, the gold flecks in the iris of Miranda's eyes, the light freckles on her cheekbone, the faint cleft in her white chin, and the downward curve of the right-hand corner of her mouth. Miranda's ankle, encased in a burnt-orange stocking, was just touching Alice's calf.

'It's so silly,' said Alice. 'Here we are fussing about spending too much money and to cheer ourselves up we go and spend more money on eating here. Oh, why aren't you eating anything? You said you were hungry.'

'I just don't feel like eating anything any more.'

'Oh well, we'll take them home with us.'

She put the two scones in her bag.

'That's not considered good etiquette,' smiled Miranda.

'No, of course not. It's thrift, and that's never considered good etiquette, is it?'

'Oh no. It's good etiquette to wait until your tailor's bankrupt before you pay your bills.'

'Mirandolina,' said Alice, 'not everyone who's upper-class can be so very wicked in every way, can they?' She put her hand on Miranda's and gently pressed her wrist. Miranda took her hand away.

'*Pas devant*,' she said. 'No, of course not. Some who are told that their tailor's on the verge of ruin look most upset and say, "Oh, I'll order a new suit." Give me a cigarette.'

Alice held the cigarette case out to her and Miranda, fumbling, took a cigarette and pushed up her veil so that it only hid her eyes.

'You don't look well, you know,' said Alice. 'Your hand's trembling like a leaf.'

'I know,' said Miranda. 'I don't know why.' She shook her head and her face suddenly crumpled.

'Oh my God, Alice,' she said in a whisper which was very low but pierced Alice. 'I don't think I can stand this thing about Anatole any longer.'

'He'll get used to it,' said Alice. Her voice was rasping. She hoped it sounded firm. 'He's always been going to bed with other women since he married me, not that I mind but I'll do the same if I want to.'

'So you've said, Alice, but it doesn't really solve anything, does it, just to keep on asserting that? Especially as Anatole agrees and still looks at us in that awful way.'

'Mother of God, that man's a brute,' said Alice. She wiped her nose on the back of her hand, took hold of Miranda's arm and would not let it go. 'He says he quite understands, but he resents us so much and when I ask him what he really wants me to do he won't tell me. He's torturing me. If he told me he wanted me to give you up and him to divorce me and marry you and go abroad or something, it wouldn't be so bad.'

'Alice, don't shout, everyone's looking at us.'

'They can't touch us. What do you care about them?'

Miranda said nothing. She was slowly crying. 'I don't want to sleep with him,' she said at last, 'but perhaps if I did it might make it better.'

Alice stared. 'You can't mean that,' she said. 'I mean, perhaps you're right, because for sure he wants to go to bed with you himself. He's human, after all.'

Miranda smiled.

'But Mirandolina,' Alice continued, 'you couldn't just give in like that. For the love of God, why ever should you? He's just jealous and possessive and peeved because you don't want to sleep with him. It's not as though he loved you. Look, he's just like all the people you ran away from — he's trying to force you to do what he wants, and I damned well won't let him.'

'Alice, aren't *you* possessive? Would you like it if I did want him as much as I want you?'

'I — no, you've got me there, I suppose.' She stroked Miranda's arm. 'I don't want to be part of a triangle. Neither do you, surely. It's just him.'

'He doesn't want to be part of a triangle,' said Miranda. 'Will you just look at the lot of us. What we all want is to sleep with the two others, and for those two to have nothing to do with each other,' she sneered. She was still quietly crying.

'That's not true,' said Alice. 'None of us has ever said anything like that. I don't know what you're talking about — why, you're asking me to believe you're bitch enough to want to split up me and Anatole.'

'Alice, sometimes I think you're about twelve years old.'

'What do you mean? Thank heaven you've stopped crying, darling,' she added.

'I mean,' said Miranda, 'that, like a child, you're incapable of believing the worst. You've got to have your world safe. It's contemptible. You've never rebelled against anything, Alice, have you?'

'I never had anything bad to rebel against, that's why,' said Alice. 'You talk as though rebelling were something necessary to people — to their souls almost — instead of the result of the wrong pressures.'

'It is necessary,' said Miranda. 'You've got to learn to criticise — I mean criticise yourself, and the things you like, and the people you love, as well as everything you've been brought up to dislike. Oh yes, you're very reasonable when your emotions aren't involved; you pointed out my crude generalisation about the upper classes just now. This is a fault of mine too, of course, I'm not denying that. But because you love me you refuse to see that I am absolutely filthy, entirely selfish, incapable of giving anyone real unselfish love.' Her voice was shaking as she crushed and stretched and tore her handkerchief. 'Don't interrupt. It's quite true. I am the greatest bitch that ever lived. If you can say, "I love the greatest bitch that ever lived, I love Miranda," that's fine, but you say, "I love Miranda, who is almost perfect," and what will happen when you realise what I really am? You'll hate me, and I just can't bear it.'

'I don't know how you can begin to say these things,' said Alice. 'Honest to God, it amazes me. You have more courage and more honesty than anyone I've ever met.'

'Honest? My God — look, this is the first time in my life I've ever been honest about myself and how loathsome I am, and you object to it. You won't see the truth, just like a child won't see that its parents don't love it, that they're in a conspiracy to deprive it of individuality, that that's their purpose.'

'I don't believe anyone consciously thinks that,' said Alice. 'Oh, Mirandolina, I can't do anything except whisper to you here, and even if we were at home and I hugged you and did anything you want, you make me feel now that there's nothing I can do.'

She paused and she dropped Miranda's arm.

'Are you telling me that you don't love me, Miranda?' She watched her. Miranda's face was white, the whites of her eyes were shining.

'You see, you see, now you're beginning to see. Soon you'll realise quite how hateful I am.' Miranda shuddered. 'It's for you to decide if I really love you,' she said, 'but I promise you, I think I love you more than I thought I'd ever love anyone again.'

'Again?' said Alice. She did not know what else to say. She clutched Miranda's hand again and questions rushed through her mind as Miranda continued.

'I loved my mother before I realised that she was exactly the same as the rest of them, out to persecute me,' said Miranda. 'But that's irrelevant. I've told you about my childhood and God help me if I should become a bore as well as all my other crimes. Alice, you're so beautiful. I wish you could see yourself now, you'd want to make an "allegory" of it. You're so pure, that's what it is, you're so much one person. You know what's right and you'll fight for it whatever happens. You're a real knight in shining armour,' said Miranda, and she was not really mocking. 'Like a child who takes rabbits out of traps. No child will believe you if you say the rabbit does damage, all they see is an animal in pain. The great thing about you is that you're not complicated, Alice. You don't have any doubts. You believe — you're a natural Catholic. How it's possible to go to mass and confession regularly and be an anti-clerical I don't know, but you manage it and I love you for it. I'm sorry, I'm not explaining myself very well. I'm just trying to see why I do love you when I don't love anyone else. Goodness,' she said, 'I love you for exactly the quality I was deriding a few minutes ago.' She smiled with an elderly, academic pleasure.

Alice was gazing at her, her mouth slightly open. 'You looked just like my mother then,' she said. 'I'd never noticed the resemblance before.' She paused. 'I can't keep up with what you're saying. So far as I can tell, you're saying I'm a simpleton.'

'Of course not,' said Miranda.

'You were saying that I'm childlike. I know that to you the word child is a terrible insult. You say it means stupid, dependent, slave.'

'I wasn't saying that you're childlike in that sense, in the usual sense. I suppose I mean in the William Blake sense. He admired and supported children.'

'Would you like some more cake?' said Alice. 'You seem to be feeling better now you're talking.' Miranda laughed. 'Well, how can you be so very horrible as you're making out if you can laugh at yourself?' said Alice.

'Now that is actually true,' said Miranda. 'You've really made me feel better. Far more than by your passionate nonsensical defences. My darling.' She put up a hand and nearly stroked Alice's cheek. Alice quivered, although Miranda withdrew. 'It's odd that a woman as intelligent as you should see everything in such black and white terms,' she said. 'You behave as though Anatole was quite perfect until he found out that you and I were having a full physical relationship — as you *said* you didn't have one with Liza or the other models,' she added quickly, '— and now this man isn't Anatole at all, it's a sort of demon who's taken on Anatole's form. You can't see that your Anatole could be jealous as well as thoroughly charming and usually tolerant.'

'You're talking about Anatole being jealous, but if you really doubt my word about how I've never been to bed with another girl apart from you, I call that insane jealousy.'

'Alice, don't start, I do believe you, of course I do,' hissed Miranda. 'I'm just a bitch, as I told you. I have to snipe. I'm sorry.' She began to cry again.

'You know,' said Alice, 'all the unpleasant sides of your character really come from your hating yourself. You've got to learn to love yourself, Mirandolina, then you'll be able to do anything . . . Oh darling, don't, please . . .' she said, as she looked up and saw Miranda's tears. 'Holy Mary, you're so damned difficult to live with. One minute you're being perfectly rational, then you're in a screaming temper, then you're affectionate, then you dissolve in tears of self-pity. Why can't you be consistent? Even Finola isn't as temperamental as you, though one never knows what she's about.'

'How dare you accuse me of self-pity,' shouted Miranda.

A waitress came up to them and muttered, as she took away their tea cups, 'Excuse me, ladies, you're upsetting the other customers.'

'Oh, all right, we'll go then,' said Alice, and she pushed back her chair fiercely and grabbed her hat and coat.

Miranda followed her into the street. 'How can you be rude to people like that?' she said. 'It's terribly unfair.'

'Oh, of course, one should always be polite but firm with inferiors,' sneered Alice.

'That's not the point,' said Miranda.

'Mother of God, you'll never teach me upper-class manners. And in any case, I thought you were trying to rid yourself of them.'

Alice walked off. Miranda, who was wearing high-heeled shoes, hurried after her with difficulty. She had paused for a moment outside Lyon's, her hands over her face.

'Alice — Alice, darling, we mustn't quarrel. It's such a terrible, terrible waste of time.' She looked up at Alice's hurt, boyish face. 'Please forgive me for anything that's wrong with me,' she finished. Her voice was very quiet.

Alice embraced her fiercely, in the middle of Bond Street as they were, and Miranda did not look embarrassed, but she did not look happy.

'I said that the only thing that's wrong with you is that you don't like yourself . . . Mirandolina, you talk as though our time is limited!'

Miranda shook her head.

CHAPTER 19

—◆—

BRYANSTON SQUARE
MARYLEBONE
May 1926

The preview of Alice's exhibition was being held in the middle
of the General Strike. At Bramham Gardens, everyone was
getting ready to go to it. Alice looked very handsome and very
tall this evening. She had had her hair cropped and wore
earrings and a short skirt, all of which suited her, and all of
which alterations in her appearance Miranda had advised.

'Finola, aren't you coming?' she asked.

Finola was sitting in the corner of the kitchen, reading
Peveril of the Peak. The household had clubbed together at
Christmas to buy her the complete works of Sir Walter Scott
in a cloth-backed edition, and she was re-reading them
already. 'No,' said Finola. 'I've seen all the paintings, and
none of the ones I like are in it.'

Alice was too happy to be irritated at Finola's taste, and
went out to join Miranda and Liza in the hall.

'I don't blame you,' said Anatole quietly to Finola. 'I'm
suffering agonies of jealousy for her success.'

'Are you?' said Finola, looking up. 'Why don't you stay
here too, then?'

'She'd be so upset if I didn't go. And I am glad for her too,
of course.'

'Anatole, you're so kind sometimes that it's annoying,'
said Finola.

'It's irritating to you because you recognise your own
inadequacy in that respect,' Miranda interrupted.

'Bitch,' said Finola. Miranda shrugged.

'Mother of God, don't you have a quarrel now! Come on, we must set off now if we're walking.'

Except for Anatole, who could not walk long distances, they were all walking to Bloomsbury, where the gallery was, to show that they supported the General Strike and would not use services run by supporters of the Government.

Miranda was not wearing a veil. Liza, Alice and Miranda walked abreast, and the two men, Volodya and Charlie, tailed behind them. Volodya's eyes were fixed on Miranda's laughing head. Unknown to Alice and Anatole, Miranda had gone to bed with Volodya, but only once. She refused to do so again, even when he came up to her room at night.

When they reached the gallery, many people had already arrived, and Alice was cheered when she entered. Leo staggered across the room to embrace her. She was asked to stand beneath her self-portrait to be photographed. 'No more book illustrations,' she said to Leo, clutching his hand and smiling.

'When I think of our little parties in Diana's house,' he sighed, 'all we hangers-on of the great artists and writers, trying to become first-rate ourselves . . . You've done better than the rest of us, you know. I must sit down, Alice, my legs are like jelly these days.'

Anatole stood listening. 'I shall be remembered as Alice Molloy's husband,' he said.

'Won't you be proud to be?' said Miranda, looking from picture to picture. Two had already been sold.

'No,' said Anatole, 'I wish to be a person in my own right just as anyone else does.'

'Oh, I didn't mean that,' said Miranda.

'Such a pity we couldn't have any of Miranda,' said Leo, rubbing his huge legs with his hands.

'That one's Miranda,' said Alice, pointing out a charcoal drawing of a red-cheeked girl on a bicycle, muffled up with scarves.

'I know, but it's not exactly your most impassioned painting of her.'

Alice went over to see Augustus and Clementina. 'How do you feel about your work, Alice?' asked Augustus, walking with her to a picture of a City pub. 'Are you pleased with yourself?'

'Oh, well, of course I am. Sometimes I have a thrill: I did these! But on the whole I feel that they're really good work only when I don't feel they're mine.'

Augustus nodded. 'Are there times when you can't work, and you feel that disaster has struck?'

'Yes. Those are the worst moments of my life. I never know when ideas and my skill will come back to me again. Sometimes it's days, sometimes months. I sit in front of the paper, smoking, dabbling, waiting for something to come to me. I've wasted acres of paper and canvas that way, but I can't just do nothing.'

'What a time to be discussing this, though!'

Acquaintances came up to congratulate Alice and praise her work, many fulsomely. She nodded and laughed and looked round the carefully lit room. She was quite relieved when after twenty minutes of this Mr Tuskin approached her with a long list of severe criticisms, and glad again to escape to the admiration which others bestowed on her.

'What a glorious whirl she's in,' said Anatole to Miranda.

'Isn't she? I say, you look very tired.' Miranda herself was sitting down.

'Actually, I think I shall go home now.'

'I'll come with you. I do hope Alice won't mind, but I've got frightful curse pains.'

'You shouldn't have walked all that way.'

'Well, I can't walk back, that's for sure. To hell with condoning the Government's behaviour. Do let's take an omnibus.'

They finished their glasses of wine, kissed goodbye to Alice, who did not object at all to their leaving, and were joined at the door by Liza.

It was a cool, bright-blue dusk, and Miranda drew her black shawl over her head and held it close to her. They walked to Great Russell Street to catch the bus, and stood opposite the British Museum.

'Finola says that she feels sad whenever she passes the British Museum, because, I quote, it makes her think of Metternich and Guizot meeting on the steps after the Revolutions of 1848,' said Liza with a smile.

'At least she has a good knowledge of history for someone who is not quite ten,' said Anatole.

'Sir Walter Scott's history, yes,' said Miranda.

'You mustn't be so critical, Miranda. She may grow out of her romanticism, and if she doesn't, it may give her pleasure all her life,' said Anatole. The bus came along and they got on, still talking.

'I find it so odd that Alice, as an artist, doesn't want to travel. She only knows Dorset and Oxfordshire besides London. She doesn't even want to see the great Italian works of art, except when one or two of them occasionally come to London. How I'd love to go to Florence!' said Miranda, fumbling in her purse for two pence. Something across the street caught her eye, and she leant over briefly to see it, for the conductor was standing in her line of vision.

She gave her twopence to him. He was staring at her. 'You are Miranda, aren't you? Miranda Pagett? I'm your brother Sebastian. Don't you remember me?' cried Sebastian Pagett, for he could not make head or tail of the expression on Miranda's face.

Sebastian was in his third year at Oxford, and had come down with many other undergraduates to man the London buses.

'My name is Laura Jones,' said Miranda.

'I'm so sorry,' said Sebastian, and he blushed and walked along the bus. But while handing out tickets, he continued to stare at them.

Miranda and Liza and Anatole were very white, and were trying not to look at him. 'You are Miranda, I know you are,' he insisted when he came back to their end of the bus.

'Yes, I am,' she had to whisper. She wanted to cry to get rid of the terrible stone in her throat and the feeling of nothingness in her guts, but she could not.

'When we get to the end of the run, we'll take a taxi; you must come back,' said Sebastian, quite gently. 'Mother's been so worried, Miranda,' he added.

Miranda nodded. As soon as he had gone upstairs she said, quite oblivious of the other people on the bus, 'We've got to make a run for it! Quick!' She pushed Anatole and Liza.

'Darling,' said Anatole, 'there's a policeman over there.

We can't. We'll just have to argue with your parents.'

'No!' moaned Miranda. 'No, no, no, I'll kill myself, I'll get off this bus and throw myself under it, and Sebastian will have murdered me!'

'Don't, Miranda, please. You're making it so much worse,' said Anatole, crying and holding her down.

Liza looked miserably round the bus at the curious, stupid-looking faces of the other passengers. She handed her hip flask to Miranda, who took a swig. Anatole took it from her.

They sat in silence as the bus drove slowly to Putney, where the journey ended. None of them could think, and they could think of nothing to say.

At Putney, Sebastian persuaded one of his friends to take over the bus, and then he rang for a taxi. In the taxi, he studiously avoided Miranda's gaze, which was no longer bewildered, but one of quiet hatred. Every ounce of Miranda's energy was being spent on not crying. Hyde Park Corner — Marble Arch — Great Cumberland Place — Bryanston Square — closer and closer — number 129, number 131 — they arrived, and the door opened at Sebastian's knock. They went into the cold brown hall with the massive, low-slung Victorian chandelier hanging from its ceiling, which as a child Miranda had attempted to touch, standing on the pillar at the end of the banisters. She was still not crying. She stood close to Anatole and Liza. The maid was new and did not recognise Miranda.

'Mr Pagett, we wish to be alone for a little while,' said Anatole. 'And there is someone whom we must ring up at once.'

Sebastian showed them into the dining room and pointed to the telephone. He did not look any of them in the face, and left the room at once.

'We could have made it,' said Miranda in a high, tight voice. 'You damned fool, Anatole. The policeman didn't know what was going on, I could see he didn't. I've been presumed dead for a year now.'

'Miranda, don't you see? We could have been traced, and then not only would you have been taken back, but Alice could have been accused of kidnapping you and brought to trial. Our best hope is to persuade your parents to let you alone now. To have fled would only have made things worse. What we must say is this: that we have always known you as Laura Jones, that we have never heard of Miranda Pagett, and that Alice has simply been employing you as a model as she does many other girls.'

'Mother of God, do you think Father's a complete fool? He'll never fall for that!'

'But Miranda, won't he be anxious not to have a scandal?' said Liza. 'If he is, he won't try to take Alice to court.'

'Exactly!' screamed Miranda.

'I'll ring Alice,' said Anatole. He rang Bramham Gardens, but Finola said that Alice was not yet back. It was much earlier than they had thought. He rang the gallery.

'Oh hello,' said someone sleepily on the other end. 'Who is it?'

'Anatole. Alice's husband. Get Alice quickly.'

'Alice Molloy?'

'Of course, fool.'

'No need to be offensive, old chap. She's just going.'

'Get her, for God's sake, before she goes!'

There was a long wait before Alice came to the telephone. 'What is it?' she said.

'I can't explain now. Come here at once!'

'Where, for God's sake?'

'Number __ Bryanston Square.'

'Holy Mary Mother of God,' said Alice, and slammed down the receiver.

Liza made Miranda finish the brandy in her hip flask. She had been walking round and round the table while Anatole was on the telephone — whispering, 'Tell me it's a nightmare,' over and over, clutching her ears. They persuaded her to sit down, and not to let her father think, when he came in, that she was still a frightened child.

Sebastian was in the drawing room upstairs. When he had finished two cigarettes he reckoned that he could fetch his parents, who were preparing to go out to dinner.

He met them on the landing. 'Miranda's downstairs,' he blurted.

145

'What?' they cried together.

'She is,' he said, nodding his head furiously. 'She was on the bus. I brought her home.'

'What cock-and-bull story is this?' shouted Thomas Pagett. 'You brought her home, just like that, after she's been gone for two years? Don't talk such nonsense, boy! The child would never . . .'

'Oh no, it's not possible,' moaned Flora Pagett, and she rushed downstairs. She flung open first the study doors, then the dining-room doors. 'My own darling girl,' she murmured, standing in the doorway. 'We thought you were dead!'

'Don't faint, Flora, for heaven's sake!' her husband shouted from behind her. He pushed past her and saw Miranda, nonchalantly sitting on the fender, her chin (famous for being like that of her Yankee grandmother) held high.

Thomas Pagett blinked and said hoarsely, 'What are you doing here? Who are these?' He was almost crying.

'Let me introduce Anatole Brécu and Liza Brécu,' said Miranda, with her eyes tightly shut. 'I'm here, Father, because I was found by Sebastian, and in a few minutes, when Alice arrives, everything will be sorted out for you, but for the moment, will you just sit down and be quiet and not ask any more questions!'

'Alice? Who's Alice? Another damned . . .'

'Randa, I'm just so pleased you're home,' said Flora Pagett, very normally and deliberately. She embraced Miranda's stiff body. 'How you've changed, dear,' she continued, dabbing at her eyes with the back of her hand, like a small girl.

'Leave me alone, Mother, please.'

They waited only a few minutes, twisting their hands in silence, until Alice arrived. Every time Thomas Pagett started to speak, Miranda glared at him, and his wife, looking at her daughter, hushed him. No one looked at anyone else.

They heard Alice, after ringing the bell, arguing with the maid. Neither of the Pagetts attempted to open the door themselves. 'Let her in, Betsy!' shouted Miranda's father.

Alice came into the dining room. 'We have been waiting

for you, madam,' said Thomas Pagett. 'Now can you explain your part in all this?'

Anatole got up. 'My wife and I,' he began, 'had no idea that Laura — Miranda — was your daughter. We knew her as Laura Jones.'

'Laura — Miranda — has been my model, you see,' continued Alice, with wonderful earnestness. 'For two years.'

'And she lived with you?' said Thomas Pagett.

'Yes,' said Alice.

'Tell me, Mrs Brécu —'

'Mrs Molloy.'

'— are you in the habit of picking up children in the street and having them live with you for two years, modelling for you? Are you not curious as to where their families are? Or did my daughter tell you a pack of lies about all that? And did you not see a single one of the police notices which were pasted up all over London? Do you never read the newspapers?'

'When your daughter and I met she was fourteen, which is old enough to leave school and take a job. She said she had no family. I lost my family at that age, so why should I question that? She had no home, and we live in a communal household, so she joined us. I don't look at posters in the street, Mr Pagett, and I only ever read the *Daily Worker*.'

'I don't believe any of this,' he replied. He paused to decide what he did believe.

'Randa,' said Flora Pagett in this interval, 'were you happy with — Monsieur Brécu and Mrs Molloy?'

'Very, very happy, Mother.'

'Well, Thomas, I don't see why she shouldn't go back to these people. As Mrs Molloy said, she's old enough to leave school and have a job.' Mrs Pagett stood with her back absolutely straight and her hands clenched by her sides.

'Good God, Flora! Now listen, Mrs Molloy. Whatever the truth is, Miranda has made it quite clear that you are the ringleader in this business. I want to speak to you in my study. Flora, take these people upstairs. Miranda —' he hesitated, '— go with your mother, my dear.'

He took Alice into his study, sat down at his desk and

fiddled with his pens. 'I can prove nothing against you, Mrs Molloy. In fact, I believe that you knew perfectly well who she was, and you have been concealing her from the police. Possibly you even kidnapped her. However, let that pass. I am Miranda's father, and I am responsible for her. She is here to stay.'

'Five years you'll have to keep her in misery. Then you can't stop her coming to us,' said Alice, standing near the door.

'Please let me finish, Mrs Molloy. I will not allow Miranda to communicate with you, and I will censor her letters myself.' He walked over to the window and then turned to face Alice, but he looked at her hard face only briefly. 'You have misunderstood me. I don't want to keep my daughter in misery, as you put it. I want to see her happy in her own home, her natural surroundings. I don't think Miranda will find happiness in some sort of Bohemianism. I realise that I have made mistakes in bringing up Miranda. I wish to rectify those mistakes. I care about my daughter and I want what is best for her. She's not a child any more, but she's a very young girl and she can't know yet what sort of life is right for her.' He finished with a great sigh.

'Oh, don't be such a hypocrite. You just want her because you think of her as property.'

'I have tried to explain my position, Mrs Molloy, and I see that you are not amenable to reason. Very well, you can think what you like, but the position is as it is. Goodbye, Mrs Molloy.'

Alice took a few steps and then stopped. 'But what will you really do to her? she asked.

'I will arrange for her to go to a finishing school — either in Paris or in Lausanne. Then, of course, she will come out when she is seventeen.' He was holding the back of a chair very tightly as he spoke.

Alice turned round and walked out. There, at the bottom of the stairs, was Flora Pagett.

'Randa's with Monsieur Brécu and Miss Brécu,' she said. 'I left them alone together in the drawing room. Please, Mrs Molloy, let me talk to you for a while.' She held the dining-room door wide open. Flora Pagett was a small woman who, after twenty-four years in England, still had an American accent. Her face was heavily made-up, and her hair was hennaed. She had once had Miranda's figure, but it had sagged and softened with age and childbearing. She made Alice sit opposite her, and looked at her intently. 'I do think it's right that Randa should stay with you if that's what she wants, but —'

'You can imagine what your husband said to me.'

'Well, yes. You see, if she only had a choice, she might choose to come home. Oh, Mrs Molloy, I always knew she wasn't happy, and really it did worry me so! Thomas always said she had plenty of people to look after her, the best, trained people, so I shouldn't trouble myself about her.' She broke off. 'You can't imagine what it's been like, these last two years. She was driven to do this terrible thing to us. Maybe we deserved it. Did we?' she said, gazing tearfully at Alice.

'Yes,' said Alice.

'Everyone says that the upbringing we gave Randa never did them any harm. In New Orleans, now, we don't treat children like they do here — oh, Thomas always says I mustn't talk so much about life back home! I'm sorry. Mrs Molloy, I'm so selfish, pouring out my troubles to you at a time like this. I'm sure you'd like to go and see Randa now. The drawing room's on the first floor, on the left.'

'I don't think it was really your fault, Mrs Pagett,' said Alice suddenly.

Alice found Miranda crying in Anatole's arms, choking and screaming and red in the face. She flung herself upon Alice when she came in. 'It's too terrible, too terrible to happen!' she cried. 'What did he say to you, Alice? What did he say?'

Alice could not answer. 'Oh my little one, my own darling,' she whispered. 'He didn't say anything much. But he won't be sending you back to Radfield, that's for sure.'

Miranda calmed down a little. Liza and Anatole sat on a sofa by the fireplace, looking at their feet while Alice and Miranda clasped each other. In a way, they were all quite glad, momentarily, when after five useless minutes the Pagetts came in and Thomas Pagett asked them to say goodbye to Miranda.

They all kissed her before they left. Miranda stood there woodenly even after the door was closed behind them. Her parents said nothing.

Outside the house, they watched, as though expecting to see Miranda tearing through it, the heavy, gleaming black door. 'She might as well be in Holloway,' muttered Liza.

'Oh God, don't say things like that!' cried Alice.

'We must get home quickly,' said Anatole. He walked them to Oxford Street, where they hailed a cab.

Alice sat in the corner of the taxi, blank-faced and shrunken. She resisted Anatole's attempt to hold her, though he needed comforting as much as she did. He wished that he could go and talk to Kate, who now lived with Richard in Hampstead; but he felt that he could not leave Alice tonight.

Alice went up to her room, and she was left alone. Supper was very silent.

'She had such a lovely body,' cried Charlie suddenly. 'Her waist asked you to put your arm round it.'

'How can you be so crude about her today of all days?' cried Anatole.

'Don't pretend you're not thinking the same as we are,' laughed Charlie. Volodya was silent. 'She rejected your attentions too, didn't she? Or gave you just a tiny taste? None of us ever made it with her.'

Anatole said nothing. It was, however, less disturbing to concentrate on his unsatisfied desires than on Miranda crying her heart out in a stately bedroom in Bryanston Square once again with no one to love her and no one to love.

Miranda was at that moment simply trying to think of a detective-proof method of murdering her father.

CHAPTER 20

❧

BRAMHAM GARDENS
EARL'S COURT
September 1926

Dearest, darling Alice,
    This is the first letter I've been able to write. Father has censored all my letters and I can't get hold of stamps to write to you in secret. However, he didn't check that the letters are censored at this place!
    This finishing school is very old-fashioned. We don't learn anything remotely useful, like typing. Dancing, Italian, French, deportment, drawing and etiquette are what Mademoiselle believes is necessary. Not quite the 'use of the globes' as Jane Austen has it, but almost. Still, we are quite free. We can go out into Lausanne in the afternoon. My main problem is boredom and loneliness, and missing you. I read a lot. Father sends me books from London. I was so amazed. He said to me: 'I know you like books, Miranda, so do take any of those in the Library. I'm afraid they haven't been much appreciated since my mother died. I don't expect they'll have any of the stuff you like reading at the school, so write to me and I'll order any books you want.'
    I was sent to Lynmore with my mother two days after the disaster. We were alone together up there for about two months, and we became rather friends. I used to hate her as much as I hated Father, because although I knew, in a confused way, that she didn't altogether believe that what was being done to me was right, she never tried to stop it. But I know now that she did try. She wanted my nice governess to stay, when Father sacked her. She's told me about herself, too. She's had a sad life. Her mother took her to England when she was seventeen, intending to marry her off to an English gentleman. She was almost forced to marry Father. Grandmother didn't really know about the English gentry: she couldn't tell the difference between a

151

born landowner and a rich industrialist turned landed gentleman like my grandfather, with whom she got on very well. Father is very ashamed of his father's only being a Northern businessman who made his packet, like so many others, in the great days of Free Trade.

When I was young I couldn't see my parents like this: as worried, snobbish human beings. I can't hate them any more, now that I've been forced to understand that they're not monsters — nothing so interesting — but only the dull run of humanity. They still bore me, though, and I resent my father's assumed right to tyrannise over me, benevolent though he's making that tyranny now.

I lie in bed at night and I imagine that I'm sitting in the kitchen with you, with Palmerston on my lap. It's frightening, Alice, but the longer I'm away, the less clear the image of our life is to me, the further it recedes into a blur of friendly muddle. I try to imagine your faces, one by one, and whereas they used to be photographed on my mind so clearly that I would cry, now I can hardly visualise them. It's terrible, treacherous, in a way, that wounds do heal. One thinks they'll last forever, but they don't, however painful they are and however much one hates the pain. Dull acceptance takes over in the end. There aren't any Miss Havishams in real life, though one feels there ought to be. I ought to be sadder, but I'm not any more; I'm only bored and lonely and missing you all, I'm not ravaged by grief. I don't feel passionate about anything. I don't think I ever will do again.

I'm coming out in May. I'll be able to see you after that, because one isn't chaperoned any more. (I only found that out this summer. I had awfully vague ideas about débutante life when I was shut away from the adult world.) Perhaps that's partly why I'm not a figure of tragedy.

All my love, Alice, and write back soon.

Alice slowly folded the letter, creased it, and then unfolded it again. It had been written without a break, scrawled in places, and hastily shoved into the envelope and posted. She got up and went downstairs with it. Anatole was practising on the violin in his room.

'Never come in when I'm playing!' he shouted as the door opened.

'Letter from Miranda,' Alice said.

He read it standing, with the bow in his hand. 'It's not very passionate or very sorrowful, is it?' she said.

'As she comes near to explaining, you'd have got passionate and sorrowful letters if she'd been able to write in May and June. Did you know that she'd be coming back and coming out so soon?'

'I thought she would be. I wasn't sure.'

'*Sainte Vierge!*' he screamed, throwing down the letter, which Alice picked up. 'You mean that you have been like this — maudlin and flying into rages with us all every day — when you knew that you'd see your little darling so soon?'

'Soon! She might be dead by May. I didn't know, did I? I wasn't sure. That was the worst thing. I presumed that she'd be chaperoned everywhere, like my mother was when she was a débutante.'

'Get out. I can't endure you any more. If you really loved her, you'd be glad that she's content enough; not angry because she isn't in a continuous paroxysm of grief and anger such as *you*'ve worked yourself up into.'

Alice turned pale. Anatole watched her walk woodenly upstairs almost with glee, but when she had disappeared from view he returned, frowning, to his violin, and half hoped that Alice would come back quite soon.

Alice paced round her studio, looking at the many pictures of Miranda on the walls. She sat down, eventually, in front of a piece of foolscap, holding a pen. She looked at the paper and wrote: *Dear Miranda*.

Then she continued:

Thank you for your letter. I hope you are well. I am glad you feel all right now. I have been utterly dejected, but I needn't be now you are all right. It has been terrible without you. I miss you in bed.

She wrote each sentence individually, with large full stops between every one. She began a new paragraph.

I think your parents are trying to buy you off. Don't forget what they did to you even if they aren't monsters (which I don't believe).
With much love from Alice.
PS   Come here as soon as you can, won't you?

She folded it, put it in an envelope, and went to post it. She stood in front of the pillar box for a few moments, in the dark, vaguely tracing the letters 'VR' above the slot with her finger. She would write another letter tomorrow, a cheerful, sympathetic, newsy letter which might provide some enlivenment in Miranda's life.

'Anatole says Miranda wrote!' said Jenny, as Alice slowly opened the front door. Liza was behind her. 'Show us the letter. Has she been sent back to boarding school?'

Alice gave them the letter and went upstairs. 'I'm sorry I said that, Alice,' said Anatole, coming out of his room. 'It was cruel.' Alice shook her head.

Jenny, in the kitchen, absent-mindedly gave the letter to Finola to read. 'See?' said Finola. 'She's all right. I bet she was making it up about how cruel her parents were to her.'

Liza took the letter away from her, thinking that she heard Alice's footsteps on the stairs.

~

CHAPTER 21

BRAMHAM GARDENS
EARL'S COURT
June 1927

Miranda had to wait until she knew enough about parties to tell those from which she would be missed from those which she would be able to miss without being noticed before she could go to Alice. She went to some sort of party or ball almost every night.

One evening, she dressed in short black taffeta to go to a rather avant-garde party on the borders of Chelsea. Her parents smiled to see her coming downstairs, looking so happy, so handsome, such a credit to them. 'Enjoy yourself,' her father said.

'I'm sure I will,' she replied, and swept out of the front door.

Her parents had given her a small car for her seventeenth birthday, which the chauffeur had taught her to drive. Almost no other girl of her age was able to drive herself around London as Miranda was.

Miranda had had her hair shingled, because she wore fashionable clothes, with which heavy hair in a bun looked very odd; but she knew that her previous hairstyle had been more becoming to her strong-featured and intensely female face. She was peculiarly conscious of the missing weight on the back of her head as she drove to Bramham Gardens. She still had her own key to the house, which she wore round her neck, together with her other, more necessary keys.

She embraced everyone. Augustus and Clementina and Kate were there to welcome her home, as well as all the household. 'You do look fine,' said Alice, in tears, 'but why did you cut off your hair?'

'Oh, in a fit of temper, it was so difficult to cope with and everyone was badgering me to have it cut,' lied Miranda.

'We'd have got champagne to celebrate if we hadn't thought that the sight of it would make you quite ill after all the champagne you must have had to drink in the last month,' said Augustus, his eyes twinkling.

'Give me a big glass of stout, for heaven's sake!' laughed Miranda. 'Where's Finola?' she asked.

'Gone to the pictures,' sniffed Alice. 'Come on, tell us everything that's happened since you came back from Lausanne.'

Miranda sat down in her favourite sunken armchair beneath the kitchen window and looked at Alice, almost surreptitiously. Alice had several grey hairs now and she was much thinner, almost emaciated. Alice was thinking that Miranda's face had lost that look of something more to come which it had had a year before, although in compensation, she was more classically beautiful to look at now.

'You "came out", didn't you, Clem?' asked Miranda.

'I did,' said Clementina.

'I'm sure it hasn't changed much since then.'

'Oh my dear, you don't know! We still had daytime chaperoning then.'

'I didn't mean all that. I meant Queen Charlotte's Ball and what it's all about. Getting your daughters off your hands.'

'Marriage was my escape,' said Clementina. 'Augustus and I plotted it together. It was a moderately respectable match, so we didn't have that much trouble.'

'Nonsense, my dear, my father was a grocer,' said Augustus.

'But a very rich one. Anyway, I shocked my parents by going to live in Bloomsbury — and that was before the name became associated with all those queer people, as my mother would say.' Clementina was not much given to reminiscence on the whole.

'What are all these parties you go to like then, Miranda?' asked Alice, refilling Clementina's glass.

'All alike,' replied Miranda. 'Everyone drinks too much

and becomes disgusting. It's not like you drinking. You can swallow pints of alcohol and remain perfectly sober. But they want to get drunk, so they can do it on very little. The conversation is like nothing on earth — actually, it's nothing. If you don't know someone's name, you call them "darling". There are two adjectives: "divine" and "foul". You hear those three words in ringing tones, and everything else they say is inaudible. Really I loathe nothing so much as parties. Whoever said they were for fun ought to be hanged. The noise, the smell, the heat, the boredom!'

Alice laughed. (Undoubtedly Miranda had done something to her lovely breasts: Alice had read somewhere that fashionable women made their chests flat with tight bands.) 'What do you do in the daytime, though?' Alice continued.

'Stay in bed in the morning. Read and write letters and see friends in the afternoon.'

'Do you have many friends?'

'A few,' said Miranda.

'Are there any special set events that you go to in the London season?'

'I don't know why you want to know all this. It's too boring.'

'I want to know what you're doing.'

'Well, there was the Fourth of June at Eton last Saturday. My brother Jasper's started there. That's a sort of open day. I went with my parents. Jasper was the cox in a boat race. And then there's Ascot Week — that's racing — and Goodwood, racing again, at the end of the Season. And Henley, which is boating.'

'So what do you do in the rest of the year?'

'Oh, there's the shooting season, and then the hunting season. My parents made me go out with the guns last year, but I'm jolly well not going this. Standing around in the cold applauding some idiot who's shot one bird in two hours!'

'Blood sports ought to be banned,' said Anatole.

'I quite agree with you.'

'Did I tell you Leo died?' said Alice.

'No. Oh, Alice, I'm so sorry!'

'You needn't be. He was in terrible pain for the last few months. They couldn't do anything for him.'

'I sometimes think,' said Miranda, 'that it would be a very good idea if everyone who lived long enough was killed at the age of seventy. Painlessly, of course. Then one would know exactly how much time one would have at a maximum, and one would have very little fear of being bedridden and dependent for years. One could plan one's life.'

'Just because you're seventeen,' said Anatole. 'Thank you, but I'm forty-seven and I wish to live till I'm ninety if I can keep in good health. I've never had an illness in my life since I had rickets as a small child. Augustus thinks that deformed children should be strangled at birth, too. But where do you draw the line? I've been perfectly happy with my deformity. I can't run or walk very far, but what does that matter?'

'You can walk as far as most people would ever wish to, Anatole. Of course I'm not talking about crooked legs,' said Augustus. 'What I mean is congenital idiots and children born without arms, that sort of thing. They'd be happier dead than living in some frightful institution.'

'You're absolutely right,' said Miranda. 'Anyone who has to be kept in any sort of institution for however short a length of time ought to be killed.'

'Should you have been killed rather than be sent to boarding school?' asked Anatole.

'I'd have chosen death at the time, certainly.'

'But you're a fighter, Miranda. You ran away.'

'I didn't used to be a fighter. When I was twelve I was a meek little mouse who jumped when anyone spoke to me.'

'Come now, if you'd been as meek as all that they wouldn't have been so cruel to you. They like meek children,' said Kate.

Miranda laughed. 'Well, I remember myself as a very cowed creature, but it might be a trick of memory.'

'So your brother's at Eton now. Is he all right there?' asked Alice.

'Jasper? Yes. He's a bully. My sister Viola is at Radfield. She's fifteen, a stupid fourth-form lump of a girl who's — she boasts about it, Alice — captain of the Middle School lacrosse team. When I ran away from Radfield, my father planned to send her somewhere else, and she actually begged to stay there. What can you do with a girl like that? And at fifteen, she's a child.' Miranda paused. 'It's little Damian I'm worried about. He's only eleven, and Mother's darling. He's at prep school. He went the term I ran away from Radfield. He was such a sweet, inventive, kind boy when he was in the nursery. He hardly ever talks now. He's totally silent for two weeks before he goes back to school. It's absolutely horrible to be with him. I can't do anything about it. I've tried to persuade my father to send him to private tutors, but no, that's mollycoddling. The old brute's learned nothing.'

They ate silently for a few moments.

'Miranda, why do you hate your sister for being happy at Radfield, just because you hated it?' asked Kate. Alice had not dared to ask that.

'Because it makes her a barbarian.'

'You're so damned intolerant.'

'You would be intolerant too, if . . .'

'Aye, maybe I would, but you'll make no friends if you can't stand those who have different tastes from yourself. Is your sister a bully, or a liar, because she likes lacrosse?'

'*Elle est une brave fille*,' shrugged Miranda. 'And that's all you can say about her.'

'What does that mean?' asked Alice.

'Very nice but not very bright,' replied Anatole.

'Well, most of the people in this world are "*brave*",' said Kate. 'And you just have to get on with them as best you can. Intelligence sometimes causes only trouble.'

'Do you think I don't know that? That's been my entire experience. And doesn't stupidity cause trouble? Read *St Joan*, Kate. It's the cause of most of the cruelty in the world.'

'I have read *St Joan*.'

'Shaw is extremely overrated,' said Augustus.

'I don't care what you say, Kate,' continued Miranda, 'but stupid people ought to be simply exterminated. Or if not that, they shouldn't have any power over others. The highly intelligent should rule.'

'I'd like to know how much coal would be produced if a Cambridge professor was responsible for the mines,' smiled Anatole.

'What about Nietszche as an example of an intelligent person?' said Kate.

'Voltaire? Erasmus? Bernard Shaw? Marie Stopes?'

'Oh, just shut up, you two,' said Clementina. 'I've got a headache, and I didn't come to hear a quarrel.'

'Can you stay the night, Miranda?' asked Alice.

'I'm afraid not. If my parents ever found out I'd been out all night they'd suspect that I'd been here, and then they'd send me up to Lynmore.'

Miranda got up to go at one in the morning. She kissed goodbye to Alice in the hall. Alice was very tired that night, and went straight to bed. Anatole was still in the kitchen.

'Yes?' he said, in surprise.

She looked urgent. 'I want to talk to you alone, Anatole. Please.'

'But of course. Sit down.'

'No — would you mind coming out to the car? I'd rather we talked there, for some reason.'

'Ah, it's your territory,' said Anatole. 'All right, if you like. Is it cold out?'

'No, not in the least.'

Miranda's car was parked round the corner. She walked slightly ahead of him. When they reached the car, she got into the driver's seat and sat with her hands fixed on the steering wheel, looking straight through the windscreen, while Anatole looked at her.

'The most ghastly thing has happened, Anatole.' She fiddled with the gear.

'Don't drive me off. What is this thing?'

'I don't desire Alice any more. I've grown out of my homosexuality. Many people do, you know.'

'I've read my Freud, yes,' said Anatole. Miranda lit a cigarette. 'Is there some young man you're in love with?' he continued.

'Don't be ridiculous. Spotty chinless fools the lot of them. No, it's just as I say: I've simply grown out of being a lesbian.'

'Alice was worried, you know, that you'd no longer want her, because she looks so much older suddenly.'

'God, she could be forty from the look of her!'

'The light was not kind to her tonight. But she has aged, yes.'

'It's not just that, though. Even if she was as beautiful as she used to be, I'd still want a man — now.' She looked at him and continued, 'Anatole, I'm an awful coward, you know. I can't bring myself to tell her that I want to — to change our relationship — because she's in love with me, isn't she, and I'm so fond of her, I couldn't bear to see her pain. I feel so guilty already. I'd feel even worse if I told her myself.'

Anatole waited.

'It would come so much better from you. If she didn't actually see me while she was told . . . Anatole. If you could, I'd be eternally grateful. It would hurt her so much less if you explained, and were loving and reasonable — I'd just get hysterical, I know I would.'

'You are a coward, aren't you?' he said. He sounded merely interested.

'I told you I was!' she shouted.

There was a pause.

'But I suppose you're right,' he said. 'I'll tell her.'

'Darling Anatole, thank you so, so much.'

'You didn't used to be given to effusiveness.'

'No — but it's different now.'

'Yes, you've become a débutante. You like everything you were mocking this evening really, don't you?'

Miranda opened her mouth to argue, then closed it and admitted, with an honest smile, to a certain human fallibility.

'But I'm not a débutante inside,' she added.

'No one is a débutante inside, Miranda.'

'All right. But what I mean is that most of us Bright Young Things wouldn't appreciate someone like you. You are marvellous, you know. I'm being effusive towards you, if you like, but so I should be. It's genuine. I mean it.'

Anatole watched her. Her coral-coloured lips were slightly parted, her black-shadowed eyes were slightly narrowed. She had only ever looked like that at Alice before, and she had used to leave her powerful young face bare of make-up.

'You want me to go to bed with you, don't you?' he said.

'Yes,' she said and she looked away from him.

'I wouldn't go to bed with you now if you were the last woman on earth,' he hissed. She stared at him, because his voice was more shocked than angry.

She no longer looked like an openly lustful woman, and Anatole felt a little calmer as he looked into her frightened, painted eyes.

'Are you so incapable of — of getting outside yourself, that you cannot see that your behaviour is monstrous?' he said. 'You come here. You see Alice and decide that she is not your adoring rescuer but an untidy, ageing bohemian. You have a general taste for men, you think, but the eligible young men available to you rather bore you, so you pick on me. You rejected me two years ago, but that does not matter. A little deformed musician is just the thing to add spice to the life of the modern young lady. So you take me out here, instruct me to tell Alice that she is not required any longer, and then expect me to be another Alice to you. Except that I shall be rather in the background, a pet to be brought out upon occasion. And you seriously expect me to fall at your feet.'

'Stop it!' cried Miranda.

'I see,' said Anatole. 'You have been told this sort of thing before. You have been told that you are a monstrous egotist, that you are incapable of loving anyone but yourself. And a year ago I would have said that the people who told you such things were lying. To think I used to believe that you were the misunderstood genius you make yourself out to be!'

He paused.

'Probably,' he said, 'you are a misunderstood genius, but that doesn't stop you being one of the most unpleasant people I've ever met. Perhaps it makes you so.' He threw open the car door and walked back to the house. On the doorstep he stopped and covered his eyes with his hands. He turned round and started to run back to where Miranda's car was parked, expecting to see her now childlike face gazing from the window. The car was gone.

Anatole could not sleep that night for worrying about what he had done to her, although he had meant what he said. The next day he received a note from Miranda, enclosed in a letter to Alice:

> *You are right. The odd thing is that I really believe it when it comes from you, and not only that, your telling me what I really am doesn't annihilate me, although I believe what you say as I don't when others tell me, because I know you don't hate me.*

'Funny,' murmured Anatole as he read it, '. . . that this fundamental confidence should make her so attractive and so repellent at once.'

'What?' said Liza.

'Miranda.'

'Oh yes,' said Liza.

'Spoilt little devil,' said Kate.

—

CHAPTER 22

LYNMORE
CHESHIRE
January 1929

Thank you for sending a wreath to Kate's funeral, wrote Alice to Miranda on 11 January:

> *It was the only wreath; I'm afraid we didn't think of taking any. Yours looked very odd staring up from the grave before they started shovelling earth on it. Anatole threw it in — I think usually one lays them on top? It was a terrible day, purple sky and hailstones and all of us trying to keep from freezing and then feeling guilty about thinking of that when Kate was lying there. Clementina couldn't come so I had to look after both Richard and Anatole — and I kept thinking how much better Kate would have coped with two dumb grief-stricken men. It was such a shock her dying like that — perhaps I ought to have worried as she conceived so late after being barren all these years, but we were all just overjoyed. Kate was a doctor, but she wouldn't let the possibility of a disaster cross her mind, so none of us did either.*
>
> *I remember how she and I used to resent each other until that time after Finola's birth when I had that breakdown and Anatole was so bewildered — rather than furious — at my refusing to touch the baby, after I'd agreed to have her. Kate reconciled us then; she looked after me and got Anatole to get me that mindless tiring job, which was just what I needed to stop me worrying about all my problems. Kate liked me once she could help me — I think we all like people who need us, or who have needed us. It's difficult to live with someone who's so young and strong and confident that they seem to have no real need of other people. I'm not saying that everyone wants to be a mainstay to a host of nervous wrecks (though that's what Kate was good at), but it's terrible to feel that someone one knows well doesn't want one.*
>
> *All the women I've known well — Kate and Clementina and*

Aunt Caitlin and of course especially Mamma — have been people on whom others could rely, people one could always turn to in trouble. I've always wanted to be like that too but I've never managed it. I suppose I've been some help to you and Anatole at times, but I've been a terrible mother to Finola, and that was in spite of my trying to copy in every way my own mother, who was the best mother in the world. She never interfered, never ordered me around, but she guided me gently and she gave me so much love. I always knew she loved me, although she always treated me as though I were just another one of her close circle of friends. I thought that if I just imitated her I couldn't go wrong with Finola. Of course I knew I'd always be an inferior version of Mamma because apart from anything else she was so brilliantly intelligent. I don't really question or reject anything that I wasn't brought up to reject. I can't think things through for myself.

Sometimes I think that my fault was in trying to impose my own thoughts on Finola. Sometimes I think that my mistake was that I didn't guide her enough. I don't know and she doesn't know and we can't do anything about it; and I want to do something so much, though now Fin isn't interested any more. She's really been taking off on her own recently, spending a lot of time with her friends and becoming increasingly like them as far as I can see. I'm not saying she's mindlessly conventional, as I used to think — after all, she wasn't brought up to be as she is and so she's made her own decision against us all. She's terribly realistic and sensible — she sees through things as Mamma used to and I never could. She's nearly as beautiful and nearly as intelligent as Mamma, and I do love her but somehow I can never bring myself to tell her. I imagine myself telling her, I can picture it — and Fin looks almost shocked, in my fantasy, at my saying that.

Anyway, there's nothing to be done now. Fin's nearly thirteen, and she's got her own life. Whatever we've done wrong, we haven't made a snivelling dependent out of her, although when she was a small child she was so clinging, and I thought, backward.

I take the Sketch *and the* Tatler *now, to see what you're up to. You're terribly reticent about your friends, as though you think I'd dislike them just because they're rich and like a good time. After all, you're one of them, and I like you . . .*

She does not say 'I love you', thought Miranda — because I refused to take up with her where I left off eighteen months ago.

But all the same, Miranda thought that Alice probably *meant* love.

I only wish I could meet one or two of your new friends, continued Alice, and Miranda frowned slowly to herself:

although I'd understand if they wouldn't like me. Oh dear, that sounds almost resentful and spiteful, although it's not meant to. I think I'd better leave off personal subjects; I'm using my letters to you almost as a sort of diary, because no one will hear except you but you will *hear, and I wouldn't want to write in a book which no one will read till after my death, and then it'll be the wrong person. How I do run on.*

The weather is all right down here. I sold two paintings quite well recently. Anatole still hasn't found a job yet and is very unhappy about it, but he's got hopes of finding a place in another restaurant band — that was the sort of job he was hoping to avoid, of course, poor darling. Everyone else is fine, and we all send much love.

Alice

As usual, this letter had been quickly written and hastily posted; Alice had not gone back to correct anything.

Miranda was sitting at the little satinwood bureau in her sparsely furnished, pale-green room at Lynmore Hall, in Cheshire. It was twenty to six in the evening, in the middle of the short but empty interval between tea and drinks, during which Miranda usually wrote her letters; for she lived in the country as she lived in London, and was rarely out of bed before midday or in bed before four in the morning. She was wearing an old dark emerald green smoking suit of which her parents disapproved.

She yawned and frowned again at the letter. She too began to write, as though Alice were her intimate friend, her diary. She detailed her business; she wrote out clever remarks for future reference; and she confided.

Dearest Alice, she began:

So lovely to get your letter. The weather is foul up here and we're en famille *at the moment so there's absolutely nothing to do except read — once I start reading I can't stop but after the Season it takes me at least two months to pick up a serious book and then get into the*

*routine. I'm coming down to London in ten days' time and would
love to see you then . . .*

She consulted her diary to check that she had no social
engagements and then she gave Alice a date.

*Darling, why ever are you fussing about your treatment of Finola,
who only wanted a nice strict nanny and a few friends of her own
age — although God knows, if she'd had that, she'd probably have
rebelled and kept on rebelling. You are not your mother, and you
could never be 'an inferior version' because you've got qualities of
your own which she didn't have and which you can't eradicate. You
must realise, with your reason if not with your emotions, that she
wasn't perfect — though what chance did reason ever stand against
the needs of the* body?
 I do agree with you that Kate and Clementina are (was, of
course, in Kate's case — *I am so sorry) admirable women, and
Caitlin is a superb old lady. I was told by one old chap who'd
known her forty years ago that she used to be a real virago — but age
mellowed, evidently. Clementina is thoroughly human, but you
know Kate and I never got on. But I don't understand how you
could want to be* like *them. There is this aura of municipal
socialism and cold baths, combined with a bit of clean honest sex,
which hangs about them and* braces *one for the Fabian future.
They're converts, you see, and one used to get the odd gleam of
fanaticism from Kate. But you've just got your happy, muddled,
inherited beliefs, and that's so much more comfortable. Really, it's
better for others if one just publicly adheres to beliefs one grew up
with without actually abiding by them, instead of making a great
fuss and abandoning them in favour of what one thinks is the truth.
So long as people keep thinking like that we'll never have Church
disestablishment!
 You must be shocked to hear me talking like this, darling. The
truth is, I don't know what I think — I expect I'll be half a Whig
and half an anarchist for the rest of my life (no doubt I'm grossly
misusing the terms). What I really care about is comfort, but I want
everything else too. That's why I'm so looking forward to being
twenty-one, when my father will settle some money on me. I can see
it all, it keeps me going to think of it: twelve hundred a year and a
flat in Chelsea looking over the river, meeting only the people I really*

want to see, no questions asked by anyone — *because I'm certainly not going to tie myself down to some man. Then I can see you often.*

I want a job, too. Something in the decorating line. I supervised the doing-up of this incredibly hideous house last year and I sometimes feel that I can move mountains because I did manage to get a little light and simplicity and what-all into this gloomy monument to Self-help. However, I doubt my experience would qualify me for designing materials from ten till four in a little cellar beneath some chic shop in Bruton Street. I only planned the redecoration because my father decided he'd had a financial crisis and a professional would be too expensive though we had *to get rid of some of the worst horrors. Now every time a guest who hasn't seen the new decor arrives and looks surprised he can say in hushed tones, 'Miranda did it,' and wait for him or her to look sympathetic. Most of the dear old things do.*

Actually I don't think the redecoration is a success because no one's happier in the new house than they were in the old. The most important thing about a place is how people feel about it — your Aunt Caitlin has all sorts of beautiful valuable things jumbled together higgledy-piggledy in her sitting rooms, and the Bramham Gardens kitchen is mostly unwashed plates and cats' cushions and books and God knows what-else, and the sweet nurserymaid I used to have who lives in the lodge now has the most repulsive 'Present from Margate' type ornaments — but it's what you all want *that makes each room beautiful. Good taste is all rot — I've got it, but it doesn't make my rooms beautiful.*

I'm afraid I'm feeling rather low at the moment. The hordes are descending on Friday and their presence may drown even Damian's end-of-the-holidays misery, though to me that's always a weight on the stomach. He still doesn't know that I ran away — the story is amnesia, as you know. I'm sure both my parents think he'd leg it if he had an example, and if he's still got the spirit he had in the nursery, he will anyway — but if he was discovered he'd be far worse treated than I was because it matters so much more if a boy doesn't show the stiff upper lip.

All my love, Miranda

At seven o'clock Miranda changed into a dark brown silk dress which reached her ankles. She brushed her hair, which she was now beginning to grow — like most other young women of fashion, who had all worn short hair for the last five years. Round her shoulders she wrapped a very unusual, heavy embroidered shawl. She left her room and started to wander through the narrow, dark-panelled, thickly carpeted corridors towards the family sitting room. The corridors reminded her of a luxurious old-fashioned railway carriage: she had not managed to have them redecorated as well as the rooms, because of the expense.

At drinks and at dinner none of the family said much. Flora Pagett made the odd remark and received polite responses and cool replies. Usually, Thomas Pagett was fairly talkative at dinner, even alone with his family, and he talked chiefly of politics. Parliamentary politics was the only subject about which he knew more than did Miranda, in which she was actually interested. Tonight, he was looking down at his plate, only pausing to frown at his wife's remarks and to glance at Miranda, when he was sure that she could not see him.

After dinner her brother Damian went up to bed and the rest of the family retired to the small sitting room. The men did not remain in the dining room, because Miranda's father and her sister Olivia's husband did not have much to say to each other. Miranda started to play mah-jong with Olivia and her husband and her brother Jasper. Her sister Viola put a record on the gramophone and played it very quietly so as not to irritate her parents over much. The butler came with brandy, port and cigars on a tray. Thomas Pagett quickly poured himself some brandy, then remembered to offer something to Olivia's husband. He thought that brandy and port and cigars were not for women, but tonight he asked Miranda, very nicely, whether she would like a little port and a cigar.

'Thank you, Father,' said Miranda. She looked at him and he turned away to pour her some port.

Presently Jasper called mah-jong. Thomas Pagett got to his feet.

'Miranda, if you don't mind, I'd like a word with you — could you come into the study for a moment?' he said, straightening his tie.

'Of course, Father,' said Miranda. She followed him down

the cold passage. Her father flung open the study door and just remembered to allow her to precede him. He watched her glide through. She looked very calm and bored and beautiful.

Miranda was hurriedly rehearsing in her head the conversation which was about to take place, about her enormous dressmaker's bill. She looked round the study. This room was filled with various pieces of furniture which had, by some accident, not been discarded when the house was restored in 1873. The portraits on the walls were all of the Fitzwilliams, into which old Catholic family Thomas Pagett's father had married.

'I've paid your bills,' said her father. 'Your dressmaker's bill was fairly steep but you seem to have been economising in your hats — very modest bill from your milliner. I want you to dress well, you know — I mean of course you do dress well — so don't worry too much about the cost. Just as long as you don't want three diamond tiaras.'

'I thought you were still having a financial crisis?' said Miranda, opening her eyes wide.

'Well I'm not any more,' he said. 'This isn't what I wanted to talk to you about,' he said. He started to choose logs from the log-basket to put on the fire. His hands were shaking.

'Listen, Miranda,' he began, 'I could talk about this later but I'd better make it clear now. I don't — I don't want you to have too much of a shock. The thing is this: if you get married I will settle three hundred thousand pounds on you, and if you don't I will not pay you an allowance if you chose to live apart from your mother and me after you're twenty-one, nor will I leave you anything in my will,' he gabbled. He did not hear a sound from Miranda in the second or two which he took to pause. He drew his breath in quickly.

'You could have any man you liked, Miranda. You know you could. I don't know why you object to getting married, it's a quite irrational obsession, you could twist some man round your little finger anyway,' he hurried on, while Miranda neither spoke nor moved. He tried to think of more things to say.

'I see,' said Miranda, in a very soft voice. 'I have disgraced the family sufficiently already. I can't be allowed to be an old maid in addition, or, of course, to marry someone unsuitable

— naturally, you didn't need to voice that clause in the ultimatum. Good heavens, here I've been living at your expense for two years after I could have caught a husband. As it is, here I am committing the heinous crime of sleeping with any man who takes my fancy, and not even having the decency to demand payment for my services . . .'

'Stop it,' he shouted. He covered his ears with his hands. 'You're deliberately misunderstanding me. Good God, Miranda, I'm thinking of your happiness. I can't let you ruin yourself. I don't want to see you an unwanted middle-aged woman on your own. Do you think I like having to — to blackmail like this?'

'Of course, of course, Father, it hurts you more than it hurts me.'

He looked very old as he at last turned towards her again. 'How can you think that I think that about you? You were accusing me of thinking you some sort of — of high-class prostitute,' he said slowly.

Miranda started to laugh, and then she forced herself to stop. She walked out of the room.

Her father gazed. When she was out of his sight he ran to the door and shouted after her. 'Miranda!'

'I don't think we've got anything more to say,' she said and her footsteps clattered away.

In the flower room she put on her mother's fur coat. She forgot to take gloves, galoshes or a hat. Swearing, she fumbled with the key of the flower-room door and at last wrenched the door open. She left it unlocked behind her as she went out into the icy stable yard and walked as fast as she could towards her car. Shivering, she clambered inside it and jerked it into action.

The drive from Cheshire to London usually took six and a half hours, but Miranda had reached the outskirts of London after five and a half. She continued to drive very fast until she reached the top of Baker Street, and then she slowed down and started to think of the coming conversation with Alice. Until now Miranda had held the pleasant belief that her father was unable to prevent her from doing as she liked with regard to Alice, although she was not yet twenty-one. 'What do you mean you've got to marry some fool?'

Alice would say. 'Mother of God, as though you couldn't come and live with us. It's not as though we're so poor . . . you've told us you want to be comfortable financially, I know, but if you wouldn't prefer to live with people who love you than to marry someone you despise . . . you were happy here, weren't you?'

Miranda drove very slowly down Baker Street. She reached the corner of Marylebone Road and stopped. For a moment she rested her head on the wheel. She was shaking. Then she pulled herself round into Marylebone Road, and she took the last few hundred yards of her journey at over fifty miles an hour. She got out of the car in Bryanston Square and briefly looked up at the familiar house which was her final destination.

She had not brought the key to the house and she had to ring the doorbell several times, weeping with tiredness, before the housekeeper heard her and opened the door to her. Miranda barely apologised to the woman for fetching her from bed. She crawled upstairs and straight into her unaired bed. She slept until one o'clock the following day and then she drove back to Lynmore.

The following week she came down to London to see her dressmaker. She spent a very pleasant evening at Bramham Gardens, and said nothing of her new situation.

CHAPTER 23

BRAMHAM GARDENS
EARL'S COURT
March 1930

Finola was studying her face. She was standing several paces away from the mirror, squinting at her reflection. Slowly she walked towards it to see at what distance the three spots on her chin became noticeable: they could not be seen unless one was really quite close. Finola was not comforted. She stared at the spots and gingerly squeezed one. Then she opened a bottle of a new astringent and doused her face with it, though she had been told by Kate that anything other than plain water would probably do her skin more harm than good. Perhaps one day someone would want to kiss her, and he would certainly notice her spots, and then he would say a hurried goodnight instead of kissing her. Jane at school had said that this particular lotion had rid her of several spots.

Next Finola brushed her hair and wondered whether she might wash it. She brushed it very gently because it took a long time to curl it, with rags. She was saving up for a permanent wave at the moment: she had not mentioned this to anyone at home because she was certain that everyone would claim firstly that it would ruin her hair, which was probably untrue, and secondly that her hair was beautiful anyway, which was a blatant lie, for her hair was ginger, although Alice called it red-gold and said it was almost as lovely as her mother's.

Finola put on some white powder and red lipstick. The colours distracted attention from her large, soft, dark-grey eyes but she felt comfortable behind the bold lipstick. She still had half an hour before she was due to go out with the other girls to the cinema, although she was quite ready. She decided to go and see Jenny, who was in bed with 'flu'. Jenny now had her doctorate, and was a biochemist. She worked at London University.

'You look like a fashion plate,' Jenny said from her bed when Finola came in.

'Oh no,' said Finola, 'my hat's a bit too big and my skirt's too short too.'

'Well, you know all about it,' said Jenny. '*Mais tout de même, tu es très jolie.*'

They continued to talk in French. Only Anatole and his daughters were French speakers, but they did not all speak French to each other. Anatole occasionally spoke in French to all of them; Liza always spoke English.

Finola sat down on Jenny's bed.

'I wanted to talk to you about something,' said Finola, plucking at the eiderdown. 'I don't know whether I really want to carry on at school. I've spoken to Anatole and he was very understanding but he didn't give me any advice, and Alice said it was entirely up to me to decide, and she was too busy to listen. Clementina was a bit patronising. She said I was too young to know my own mind and that I'd enjoy Queen's.'

'What will you do if you do leave school in the summer?'

'That's the problem,' said Finola.

'What do you want to do eventually? Do you still want to live in the country and have lots of children?'

'Yes, of course. Why should I change my mind?'

'Well, very few people are as constant in their ideas as you are. I had absolutely no idea of what I wanted to do until I was fifteen or sixteen, and plenty of people go to university and still don't know what they want to do after that. Do you know why you've always wanted that so much, Fin?'

'I suppose loving children is just nature,' said Finola, 'not just children but helpless things. Everyone responds to people who need help.'

'So long as they know they need it. Most people never see people, or things, who are badly off. That's the problem.'

Finola forestalled her. 'Now don't start talking about socialism and the class system again,' she said. 'I was saying that I don't really know why I want children so much. But I want to live in the country because I so adored those holidays at Aunt Caitlin's. I know,' she said. 'I want to be like Aunt Caitlin. I want to support people.'

Aunt Caitlin had died in February.

'It's odd you should say that,' said Jenny. 'I'd never seen Caitlin as a matriarch before. But she was, wasn't she? We all used to go up to King's Norton when we were fed up, and we all came back feeling better. And yet we never really appreciated it while she was alive. You don't think that it was Caitlin rather than the place itself that made King's Norton have that effect on you, Fin? Just because you didn't really feel her influence directly?'

'Maybe,' said Finola, 'but knowing that isn't going to stop me wanting to live in the country.'

'Do you know, the other day Liza told me that *she* wants to live in the country.'

'Liza? She's never said anything about it.'

'I know, but Liza never says much. She used to talk to Alice a bit before . . .' Jenny paused.

'I know what you're talking about,' said Finola. 'Liza thinks Alice jilted her, sort of.'

'So you do know.'

'I'm not a baby. I was actually around when Miranda was here, too.'

'Yes, you must have been hurt by it all.' Jenny wanted to see whether Finola would talk.

Finola shrugged. 'I'm going to give all my love to my children,' she said. 'All of it. So,' she finished as she got off the bed, 'you think I ought to go to Queen's?'

'Well, I didn't actually say so, but I think you ought to try it. The only thing I really would say to you is that you should remember that you're going to be a woman of means when you're twenty-one; Caitlin left you quite a bit. You won't have to marry for money to obtain your leisured life in the country.'

'Not for the money, no.'

'Liza's had to earn money,' said Jenny, 'and she hates it. You won't have to do that, either.'

'Oh yes,' said Finola, 'I'm privileged. Everyone's privileged in one sense or another. By the way, do you want anything from downstairs?'

'No, I don't think so — oh, you couldn't get me an apple, could you?'

'Hot-water-bottle?'

'That's a good idea.' She gave a luscious sniff and wriggled in the bed, realising at Finola's suggestion that she was actually cold.

'You know,' said Finola, 'I'm sure you're not really a distinguished lady academic. You just don't look right.'

Jenny laughed. 'Wait till I get grey hair,' she said, and then added, 'but the bit about "distinguished" is certainly true.'

'Oh, they just won't give you a lectureship because you're a woman and probably better than most of the doddery old men. They don't want to be put to shame.'

'You're a darling,' said Jenny, and she meant it, but Finola thought that Jenny didn't believe her.

She went down to the kitchen, filled a hot-water-bottle and took it up to Jenny together with the apple.

'You could always be a nurse, you know,' said Jenny with a smile as Finola tucked in her sheet.

'Yes,' said Finola, as she left the room, 'that's quite a good job for a girl who's not very clever.'

Finola was due to meet her friends, Stephanie and Marianne, in a quarter of an hour at Marianne's family's house in the Little Boltons, before proceeding to the West End for the matinée. She had rarely seen either of them since they had left Cressida Lake for St Paul's last summer; but Marianne had rung her at short notice with a spare ticket.

Finola looked up at the large, white, ornate house. The garden in front, bounded by a wall instead of railings, was just beginning to come to life. Two solid pillars enclosed the wrought-iron garden gate, which was left ajar; and a black and blue and white tiled path ran up to the front steps. A gleaming knocker was fixed on the dark green door. Finola could see nothing of the inside save the edges of the curtains in the windows, which were lighter in colour and weight on each ascending floor.

Finola thought firstly of the large, dirty, orange-brick

house in Bramham Gardens, with its awkward gable and grey peeling window frames, and secondly of the country equivalent of this house, which would be smaller and more comfortable than King's Norton but which might well have a Victorian greenhouse in the garden. She set her hat on her head at an acute angle, marched up the path and firmly rang the bell, which was answered by a maid.

'Fin!' Marianne shouted from over the second-floor bannisters, which were painted smooth clean white. 'We're upstairs — second door on the left.'

Finola had been here once before, and remembered the house quite well, but Marianne had forgotten this.

'I say, devastating lipstick,' said Marianne, when Finola came in, in a very good imitation of her elder sister's manner, which Stephanie recognised.

'Thanks,' said Finola. She peered at them both to see if either of them looked really sophisticated. They had both turned fifteen.

'Steph, do please finish those chocolates, you know. I'm banting and I simply can't resist,' said Marianne. Stephanie was sprawling on the bed. 'Fin, do finish them. Steph's so fat anyway and you're quite a skinny little thing still, aren't you? Just wait a year or two before you have to start worrying!'

She sighed and plumped herself down at her dressing-table as though she had been covering up wrinkles there for years. She searched in a little bag at the back of one drawer for her one lipstick: it was such a discreet colour that her parents never noticed when she was actually wearing it.

'Am I fat, Fin?' asked Stephanie, holding the chocolates out to her.

'Oh no,' said Finola, looking at the bulge of flesh which poked over Stephanie's waistband, 'not really. Just puppy fat,' she added.

'Puppy fat is babies and children,' said Stephanie, looking up.

'No it isn't,' said Finola eagerly. 'It's fat which you lose automatically as you get older. At any age.'

'I think its's about time my sister lost some of her puppy fat, then,' said Marianne. 'Just look at this dress. Miles too

177

big round the hips. And if I don't wear this I'll have to wear something about as flattering as my school uniform.' She nodded at the open wardrobe which was full of new cashmeres and lawns and lace.

'Your sister isn't fat,' said Stephanie, 'she's just developed.' She pushed out her matronly bosom.

'It's not fashionable to be developed,' said Marianne. 'You can't see how developed I really am because I've been banting so hard recently. It's taken all my weight off. Honestly, parents are the lousiest bore. I'm just as mature as Celia — where's the difference between fifteen and eighteen? But they behave as though I'm an absolute child. They even say I'm too young to bant. It really is absolutely crymaking. I have to eat simply masses and then make myself puke.' She sounded very cheerful.

Finola stared at her. 'You make yourself sick after every meal?' she said.

'*Il faut souffrir pour être belle*,' said Marianne. 'Then I eat my diet afterwards. Oranges and brown bread.'

'I think that's plain silly,' said Finola.

'I'd forgotten,' said Marianne, turning towards her. 'You always start talking with an Irish accent when you start criticising people.'

'I never do,' said Finola. 'Never. Even my mother hardly has an accent. She isn't really Irish at all, she's a Londoner.'

'A Cockney born within the sound of Bow Bells, you mean?' said Marianne, laughing.

'Yes I do,' said Finola, and flushed.

'Come on,' said Stephanie, 'we'd better be going. I suppose your mother will insist we take a taxi, Marianne. That's an awfully nice hat, Finola,' she added. She smiled brightly as she looked at Finola and used her formal name, and then she led the way downstairs.

After the film the girls went to have tea at Fuller's. Then they took a taxi back, but even so they were later than they should have been.

At Marianne's house they were scolded, as Marianne had said they would be. 'I don't know how I'm going to explain this to your parents,' Marianne's mother said to Finola. Finola looked, then, as though she had parents who were like

Marianne's mother.

Marianne's mother looked at Finola's painted mouth. 'I hope they won't mind too much,' she said.

'I don't think so,' said Finola.

'Well,' said Marianne's mother, 'what about a glass of lemonade before you go, Stephanie and Finola?'

They went into the drawing room. The drinks had already been brought in, and Marianne's father and her brother Jeremy, a Cambridge undergraduate, were sitting there, drinking whisky. They were too deep in argument to pay any attention to the girls. Marianne poured out some lemonade for the three of them.

'God, what a bore,' she said. 'They never seem to stop arguing. Honestly, neither of them will ever persuade the other one that he's right, so why do they bother?'

'You're talking as though unemployment was some sort of accident,' said Marianne's brother. 'Of course, as a pillar of the Establishment, you've got to talk like that. Anyone who hasn't got a vested interest in the social order can see that unemployment is a deliberate weapon of the ruling class, used to keep the workers where they've always been. Goodness me, one couldn't possibly let the lower orders join one in conspicuous consumption of non-necessities, could one? One might erode class differences.'

His father, who appeared to be an old man, slowly shook his head and peacefully finished his tumbler full of comforting golden whisky. Finola watched him. She had not paid any attention to Jeremy after she had heard his first comment, but she was surprised to note that his father did not look outraged or frightened at being made aware of 'the threat of the people'.

'I think,' said Marianne's father, 'that where you're really going wrong — in the sense that if you misinterpret this you'll never achieve your revolution, granting for the sake of argument that the actual facts are as you say — is in your interpretation of people's motives. There isn't any conscious desire on anyone's part to oppress the workers. The only conscious desire of the class you hate so much — of which, I may say, you're still a member — is to cling to tradition. Possibly it is a form of cowardice, but it's not an

179

evil intention. You mustn't exaggerate. I'd like you to tell me what you'd put in place of our system, Jeremy.'

'The classless society. It'll come in any case after the revolution,' he snapped.

'A society in which the classes aren't separated by income differences, you mean?'

'Of course.'

'But how can you tell that other sorts of class oppression won't come into being? Perhaps old people will be a persecuted group. Why shouldn't the categories be made according to other criteria?'

'Because all that stuff — religion and education and sex differences — is the result purely of economics. Abolish economic distinctions and all the other distinctions will vanish.'

'I can't quite accept the third instance you gave,' smiled his father, 'but still, I think you may be right if after the revolution you can stop everyone from believing in the soul. Then you might achieve your uniformity. But you'd have to do it by force, I think. You can't just abolish thousands of years of religious tradition like that. And I'm afraid I really don't believe that uniformity is desirable. People ought to be able to hold their own views and go their own way.'

Jeremy sighed deeply and opened his mouth to refute an argument which was familiar to him. Stephanie was looking in puzzlement at Finola, who, it seemed to her, looked as though she had never heard anything of this kind before.

'But are you a real Conservative?' said Finola to Jeremy's father, and then she blushed and did not know herself quite what she meant. 'I'm sorry,' she stammered. 'I really am. I shouldn't have been listening but you just don't sound at all like what I thought a Conservative would sound like and Jeremy was saying that you were one and . . .'

'Good heavens, my dear, you're getting quite upset. It's nice to see a pretty girl who takes an interest in things, you know. As to your question, I'm afraid I'm not sure myself. All I can say is that I won't destroy what we've got until I can be sure that a replacement will be better.'

'Oh, by a better replacement you just mean "the greatest happiness of the smallest number",' said Jeremy, who had just been noticing how very pretty Finola was. He did not recognise the child he had met eighteen months ago.

His father closed his eyes briefly, but not as though he were attempting to control his temper. 'I think that "all is for the best in the best of all possible worlds" expresses my views rather better. Who said that, my dear?' he said to Finola. Finola did not mind his exceeding benevolence, though she blushed again, because she thought she knew the answer.

'Leibniz?' she hazarded. Anatole was fond of Voltaire's comments upon Leibniz.

'Quite right.'

Marianne and Stephanie were staring at her, as though she were just as eccentric and radical as the rest of her family.

'I must be going. I really must, thank you for the lemonade,' she said, standing up.

'I say, are you walking? Shall I walk you back?' said Jeremy suddenly and he too blushed in front of Marianne and Stephanie.

'Oh, don't bother — oh, thank you,' said Finola and they both hurried out of the drawing room.

They walked very fast along the pavement, in silence for about a hundred yards.

'I suppose you're at school with Marianne?' he said at last.

'No,' said Finola, and she paused very slightly, knowing that she must look at least sixteen if he was walking her home. 'I'm at Queen's College. We were at prep school together.' If Marianne found out that she had said this it would not matter, because Finola was sure that she would not be seeing her again. But if Jeremy discovered that it was a lie he might abandon any plan he might possibly, vaguely, have of taking her out one day. Finola shook her head, like a dog shaking itself free of water. 'What are you going to do when you leave school?' he said.

'Oh, I'll have to get some sort of job before I get married.'

'Working-class women have to work after they get married, even when they're pregnant,' he said. It suddenly occurred to him that Finola might be shocked, or made giggly, by the use of that word: she simply looked irritated, as though she were quite used to that sort of statement. But she was relaxing, he thought; she was not quite so far apart from him on the pavement.

'Yes,' said Finola, 'and so did my mother, though she has seven hundred a year. She's an artist,' she added.

'Really? I say, what's her name?'

'Alice Molloy. You won't have heard of her.'

'Oh, I have. A chap who's up at Oxford with me's got one of her paintings in his rooms — I think it's awfully good. It's of a young girl in silhouette — you can't see much of her but you can tell the model must have been beautiful. It's just called "Miranda".'

'Here we are,' said Finola. 'Goodnight. Thank you for walking me home.' Her voice was gracious, cheerful, and final.

'Oh — er — goodnight then.' He just brushed her cheek with his lips and hurried off, casting a backward glance at Alice Molloy's house.

Finola threw her hat on to the table in the hall. So Alice had sold one of the pictures of Miranda which crowded her studio — though she had said nothing about it to anyone. True love, thought Finola, might hurt oneself and one's love object and everyone else, but it was noble and forever: the pain caused by true love was forgiveable. The pain caused by a passing fancy, such as Alice's passion for Miranda now seemed to be, was not. To Alice, of course, Finola thought as she walked upstairs, all the faults of a pretty model twelve to fifteen years old were forgiveable.

Recently Alice had been seeing and listening and talking to Finola more often than she had used to, and she had painted an exceedingly unflattering portrait of her which she said showed up Finola's interesting points quite well. Soon Finola would grow up — and then, she supposed, her feelings, like her body, would become as unacceptable as they had been when she was eight. Finola sat down on her bed and did not cry, but she hugged herself very tightly with her cold hands as though she were afraid that, unless she held them in, her reflections upon the unromantic truth would escape her, to become objects of public contempt and denial.

CHAPTER 24

WATERLOO PLACE
ST JAMES'S
May 1931

At one o'clock in the morning, Miranda rang. Alice was alone in the kitchen reading.

'Alice? Look, darling, can you come to my twenty-first birthday party? It's in a week's time, at Father's cousin's place, Martenby House, Waterloo Place. It's a formal ball. Come at about ten. I'll send you invitations. Bring Finola, she'll absolutely adore it, and anyone else who wants to come.'

'Well, of course we'll come if you like, but what about your parents?'

'Why on earth do you think I'm ringing up at this hour? Of course they don't know. It'll be a lovely surprise for them. But look, I want us to celebrate my independence on our own. Can I come to dinner with you on the 20th?'

'Certainly. Oh, Miranda, it's so wonderful to think you'll be free!'

'Yes, Alice,' sighed Miranda, and she put down the receiver.'

Alice was looking at herself in the mirror. She had on an old dirty camisole and baggy cotton knickers. Her thin legs and arms protruded, naked and greyish, from her loose greyish clothes. She had used to be very slender; now she was as skinny as she had been when a child. What little flesh she had was no longer firm. Lines had begun to appear on her fine dry skin several years ago. Her hair had started to turn grey. She preferred the grey to the previous dull brown, so she did not dye her hair even though she was only thirty-three. Because her beautiful mouth was still that of a young woman, and because her narrow bright eyes and heavy eyebrows were just as they always had been, Alice could, on a good day, look ten years younger than she was. On a bad day she looked far older.

When Miranda had been living with her, Alice had made an effort about her appearance: She had made herself eat enough, although she usually wanted less food than she needed. She had cut her hair and washed and brushed it properly. She had worn tidy, almost fashionable, clothes. Three years ago she had reverted to her old habits: she had gone back to wearing the clothes she had had during the war, and had let her hair grow again.

In a heap on the bed there lay a bright yellow silk dress which Aunt Caitlin had had made for her in 1917. It was Alice's only grand dress and she had planned to wear it to Miranda's ball tonight. She had tried it on and quickly taken it off again. Her face, without rouge, had peered dry and white over the gleaming silk and, when she had hastily rubbed on some of Finola's rouge, the rouge had stood out on her sharp cheekbones as two spots of red paint. She had nothing but the yellow to wear, unless she went in one of her summer frocks.

She tried on a blue gingham dress and realised that she must have been too old for the material and the colour and the cut several years ago. She bit her lip and stared at herself.

Anatole came in.

'There's a stain on this shirt-front,' he said. 'Have you got anything to remove it with? Oh, I thought you were going in that,' he said, nodding at the yellow silk. 'Do wear it. You always looked magnificent in it.'

'I haven't worn it for four years,' said Alice. 'And it looks terrible, really terrible now. And this looks awful too, and I'm so old, and I've nothing to wear and I can't go, I really can't!'

'You are a chicken of thirty-three, and you have the figure and the mouth of an eighteen-year-old girl, and all that is wrong is that you are a little too thin. So stop talking nonsense, and don't cry, my love.' He reached up and patted her shoulder. 'Go and ask Finola to lend you a dress, and do your face and all that. She'll know what to do.'

'Fin wouldn't lend me one of her dresses!' said Alice, staring. 'And you can't ask a pretty girl of her age to make an effort to improve an old hag's appearance. She thinks middle age sets in at twenty-one, and it's not worth bothering about your looks after that. And perhaps she's right.'

'Go and ask Finola. And I tell you that you are not old, and not even Fin thinks you are.'

'Really? Do you think Fin would?' said Alice, turning to him, and she looked very young indeed.

'Of course she'd be glad to. Sometimes I think you're afraid of her.'

'I am that,' muttered Alice suddenly, and she went out before he could reply.

She knocked on Finola's door and Finola, rather surprised, asked her to come in. She laughed.

'What's funny?' said Alice. 'Oh, I know I look ridiculous!'

'You look rather sweet — just unlike yourself. I say, I'm sorry, I wasn't really making fun of you, you know,' said Finola. 'You look as though you're in rather a bad way.'

Finola was quite ready and was putting away the various frocks which she had tried on and rejected.

'Can you lend me a dress?' said Alice. 'Please, I look terrible in the yellow.'

'That yellow!' sighed Finola knowingly. 'Everything of mine will be far too short for you, you know.'

'I know.'

'But you can if you like. What do you want?' She indicated the frocks which were strewn round the room.

'Just you choose something that won't make me look a hundred and five,' said Alice. 'You know I don't know anything about clothes.'

Finola paused and frowned a little at Alice, her small round mouth slightly open. Then she assumed the authority of a couturier. 'You must have something with sleeves,' she said firmly. 'And not too bright.'

In the end Finola chose a dark green wool day-dress. It was too long for Finola, who had taken up the hem; with the hem let down again, it was almost long enough for Alice.

'It isn't a dancing dress, though, is it?' said Alice.

'No, but you look very nice in it, don't you? And you carry off the awful things you usually wear without worrying at all, so why you can't go to a dance in a short dress I don't know. Besides, long dresses have only just come back. Three years ago everyone wore short.'

'All right, Nanny.'

Finola blushed and murmured, 'OK, I'll do your face now.'

She sent Alice out of the room with trimmed, brushed hair and with her skin coated with foundation. Alice looked quite dazed as she walked downstairs. She ran her tongue gingerly round her red-greased lips, and wrinkled her face curiously to feel the foundation ease and crack. Finola watched her from the bend of the stairs. Anatole joined her.

'If she carries on doing that, the lipstick will look like strawberry jam round her mouth,' said Finola. She laughed a little.

They followed Alice downstairs. She was looking at herself in the hall mirror.

'I'm sorry, Fin, but I'm going to take all this make-up off. I feel like a clown. No one will ever take me seriously.'

'Oh, Alice, don't be so stupid,' said Finola.

Alice went up to the bathroom while Anatole and Finola joined Augustus, Liza, Jenny and her lover Edward in the kitchen for a drink before setting off for the ball.

'Goodness,' said Jenny, who wore a short poppy-red dress, 'do you realise that, of all of us, Augustus is the only one who's ever actually been to something like this?'

'We're all débutantes,' said Liza. She was biting her nails.

'You don't look like one,' said Finola. 'You look like a period piece.' Liza wore a high-necked white blouse and a long black skirt. Liza flushed and Finola looked away.

'Then she can go as the Dowager Countess of Bramham,' said Augustus. 'Ah, Alice — have some gin.'

Alice gulped down some gin and they left the house. They all piled into a taxi for the drive to Waterloo Place, but they found, when they reached Martenby House, that they were not as late as they had feared, and had arrived with the throng. From the London mansion yellow light poured out through the windows and the open door into the street, and the chattering people basked under its beam. Almost everyone had arrived in a car; Finola could see only one other taxi amongst the rank of motors. She and Alice and Liza gazed at the men in their white ties and tails, at the women in long dresses cut very like Finola's, at the big cars, the yellow light and the wet shining street. The others walked on a little ahead.

'Miranda darling,' said a girl just in front of Jenny as they went into the hall, 'it is so lovely to come to a proper dance. Is there lovely decadent unsocialist champagne too?'

'There is indeed. I do like your dress, Tuffy,' said Miranda. She, like Alice, was dressed in dark green. She was greeting the guests as they came in: her mother and father stood near her, and were also shaking hands. Miranda looked a little dazed.

'Alice, Alice!' she called, and her parents turned round at the sound of her voice, though Miranda knew several Alices. Miranda embraced Alice very tightly, almost as though she were afraid of losing her, so that Alice muttered, 'There, there,' and blushed, and patted her on the back. Miranda also gave a flushed, tearful welcome to the rest of the party from Bramham Gardens and bade them enjoy themselves.

Flora Pagett determinedly advanced a shaking hand towards Alice. 'Mrs Molloy, I'm so glad you've come. I should have sent you a proper invitation.' She began the second sentence almost in a whisper, but finished it in a loud voice. Alice passed on to Thomas Pagett, whose eyes were now fixed on the wall opposite, and who bowed to her. His face was very white and his hands were behind his back. Once the whole party from Bramham Gardens had passed into the ballroom he held his hands still behind his back, and continued merely to nod at the guests, as he waited to attract Miranda's attention. As soon as the last of the timely guests had arrived, Miranda went upstairs; her father, after awaiting her return at the foot of the stairs for five or ten minutes, retired to the smoking room with a few elderly friends.

At the door of the great room in which the dancing was to take place, the guests were announced. Finola heard her own name boomed out by the footman: 'Miss Finola Molloy!'

She stood on the threshold and gazed into the crowd. It occurred to her that she could have had herself announced as Mademoiselle Brécu, Mademoiselle *de* Brécu.

She walked forward. She looked up at the blazing chandeliers and down at the parquet floor and avoided looking at the people's faces. She clumsily made her way to a corner and sat down. When she furtively looked round her again, she saw not one really handsome young man. She looked down at her lap and saw for the first time the crude stitches in her tight, fashionable, pearl-grey silk dress. She felt tears come into her eyes as she looked at her dress and listened to the laughter of people who knew each other. She wrapped her arms about herself and shrank into the shade.

Finola spent about ten minutes sitting there. She caught sight of Jenny's red dress in the crowd and hoped that Jenny would notice her. Jenny disappeared from Finola's view.

Just after the dancing began, two middle-aged ladies came to sit near Finola. There were plenty of chairs, and many elderly women were standing, talking loudly and even dancing; but Finola now felt that she ought not to be seated. She dragged herself to her feet and looked up. She put a lively expression on her face so that she would not be taken for the shy child who had been crouching in the corner. Suddenly Finola saw a blond, tall, beautiful man standing near one of the windows, several yards away from her. She felt her cheeks grow red as she inched her way inconspicuously around the walls. When she was only a few feet away from the lovely young man someone said: 'I say — care to dance?' The speaker was a gangling boy, who had a pimple on his nose. He was breathing loudly.

'Oh — oh, I never dance — oh, yes, all right,' said Finola. She saw that the handsome man was talking to a very pretty girl. 'I'd be glad to,' she muttered, still blushing, and she and her new partner shuffled away from the wall without looking at each other. A little later Finola decided, as they attempted to dance, that he was really very plain; but she still wished that she had more bosom, and hoped that he could smell her new scent.

She saw Liza looking through the dancers with her pale grey eyes, a faint smile on her lips. Liza was sitting quite calmly by the wall and she appeared not to notice or care that a dowager who was talking to the woman sitting next to her wished for her seat and was glaring at her.

A little later, Finola passed Jenny on the dance floor. Jenny was dancing with a dark, stocky man who had bright black eyes and a slight French accent.

'May I ask your name, mademoiselle? Or is it madame?' he said to Jenny. 'Mine, by the way, is Henri de Saint-Gaël.'

'Jenny Brécu,' she replied, 'and I'm not married — not officially, that is.'

He laughed and continued in French. 'You are a bohemian, then. Do you paint pictures or write novels, or do other bohemian things?'

'No, I lecture on biochemistry at London University.'

'I never thought I'd dance with a university don!'

'I never thought I'd dance with an aristocrat.'

'*Touché*, mademoiselle.' He looked at her. 'Was that contempt I saw in your face when you pronounced the word "aristocrat"?' he teased. 'Are you very, very Bolshie?' He lingered proudly over the expression and Jenny laughed.

'I'm a communist, but my life's too comfortable for me to be very ardent, so you needn't worry. And besides, Miranda was telling me that it's quite the done thing to be rather to the Left nowadays.'

'Ah, Miranda! She refuses to be fashionable in anything except her language and her dress. I believe that, before others followed her example, she herself was rather Bolshie?'

'So I've heard,' said Jenny. 'Are you married?'

'I am widowed,' he replied, 'a long time ago. In France, you know, one rarely marries for love; but, like Miranda, I like to be unconventional.' He smiled.

'Oh,' said Jenny simply. He looked almost disappointed, for she changed the subject completely.

Alice and Anatole were dancing together. Alice had twice danced with someone else, but Anatole had been leaning against the panelled doors, watching, glowering as though he hated dancing, with his twisted leg hidden behind his straight one.

'I didn't know you could dance,' said Alice, as he pushed her legs into the right steps with his knee.

'Oh yes, if I'd been a little taller, just a little of course, I could have been a lounge lizard,' he laughed. 'If you play the piano in a night club you tend to learn how a dance goes,' he added and shook his head.

'My love,' said Alice.

He smiled and said, 'Do you mind if I don't stretch up to your shoulder but put my hand on your elbow instead?'

They danced in silence for a while, holding each other quite tightly as Anatole guided them around the other couples.

'We've been married fourteen years,' said Alice, 'and we've never danced together before.'

'Good heavens,' said Anatole. 'I have heard a sentimental remark from the lips of Alice Molloy!' They both laughed and held each other even more closely, as they had not done amongst their own friends for ten years.

Someone tapped on Alice's shoulder as she was looking down into Anatole's face.

'You make an awfully pretty couple,' said Miranda, 'but I loathe dancing myself. Won't you come upstairs and meet a few of my friends?'

'We haven't met any of your friends before,' said Anatole.

'I know,' said Miranda, raising her eyebrows, 'that's why I want you to come now.'

'Let's go,' said Alice, and after a moment Anatole followed Alice and Miranda.

Miranda and her friends were occupying a small sitting room on the second floor.

'Sweet of Aunt Helena to give us her retreat,' she remarked as they went upstairs. 'I decorated it for her, you know. I mean I didn't just choose the stuff, I was pasting paper and all that. I was paid one and six an hour,' she said. 'I've tasted real life.' She gave her old twisted smile.

'I've heard that a lot of Bright Young Things are taking jobs nowadays,' said Anatole.

'Oh yes,' said Miranda. 'Running restaurants for one's friends, and being a mannequin, and that sort of thing. Such fun. No real reason why it should assuage one's conscience about the unemployed, but it seems to.'

The room was decorated in silver-grey and cream, and filled with delicate, painted, late-eighteenth-century furniture. There were dark colours and bright colours in the rugs which covered the plain polished floorboards.

'It's beautiful,' said Alice.

'Let me introduce Alice Molloy and Anatole Brécu,' said Miranda to her interested friends, as Alice and Anatole stood just inside the doorway. 'The truth about my disappearance,' she continued as she guided her exhibits to the sofa, 'is that I ran away from school deliberately and lived with these two for two years.'

One or two people's faces fell. It had been rumoured that Miranda, who was famous for her amorous disposition, had been a white slave, a child prostitute, and had rather enjoyed it.

'So why have you decided to spill the beans at last, old thing?' said Tuffy, whose face had fallen.

'Because I'm twenty-one, and able to introduce them to you.'

'I still don't see why you wouldn't tell us before.'

'Darling, it's not very exciting information, is it? Not nearly as exciting as the enigma of my disappearance. And my respected father naturally wished my association with the bohemian world to remain a secret. I'm celebrating my twenty-first birthday by breaking trust and telling you.'

'Can I gossip?' said Tuffy.

'Not yet,' said Miranda.

'You're an artist, aren't you, Miss Molloy?' said a young man called Toto Howard.

'I paint,' muttered Alice. She hated being addressed as 'Miss Molloy' now that Mr Tuskin was dead.

'Yes,' said Toto, 'you paint rather erotic pictures of young girls, don't you?'

'I hope so,' said Alice. She blushed under his sophisticated gaze, though she was not embarrassed.

Anatole picked up her hand and squeezed it, as he usually

did when she was getting irritated.

'Yes, Toto darling, I had a lesbian love affair with Alice when I was her model,' said Miranda, smiling. She watched him blush.

'I've read *The Well of Loneliness*,' said a girl with a round, kind face. 'I thought it was awfully good.'

Alice looked at her. 'Yes,' she said. 'It's a brave book to talk about something which people refuse to see exists. There isn't even a law against lesbianism.' ·

'Oh yes,' said Toto brightly, 'because none of Queen Victoria's ministers could bring themselves to explain it to her!'

Anatole laughed. 'I hadn't heard that story,' he said.

'Oh yes,' said Toto, 'it's quite true.'

'Alice,' said Miranda quietly, 'you don't look happy. Shall I fetch Augustus to make you laugh?'

'I'm all right,' said Alice. 'I was just thinking that your life must be very dull, really.'

'You knew that before,' said Miranda.

'I used to *believe* it,' said Alice, 'not *know* it.'

'Look at Anatole chatting up Tuffy,' said Miranda. 'He can talk to anyone, can't he. I know that look on her face. He'll be her grand passion for the next three months, poor darling.'

She was watching Anatole and Tuffy as she stood by Alice's side. Slowly she turned her head round to look at Alice. She looked into her eyes only very briefly.

'Why did you invite us?' said Alice.

The side of Miranda's mouth twitched. 'I'm sorry,' she said. 'I really am. I don't know. Can't you enjoy yourself?' She started to tease. 'Can't you even enjoy making us feel guilty about the Unemployed?'

'Darling, isn't the point of giving a ball to make us forget about the Unemployed for a tiny while?' called one girl. Miranda smiled.

'No,' said Alice. 'I never talk about all that any more. I've no right to talk about it, I'm not a worker. I'm as much a parasite as you, only I'm more hypocritical, that's all.'

'Let's talk when I come to Bramham Gardens,' said Miranda. 'Do let's.'

'All right,' said Alice, 'and I'll stay now if you like.'

'Please.'

Miranda's eyes were fixed on Alice's mouth. Alice felt an old sensation as she looked up at Miranda's dark eyes and her creamy skin. Then she noticed that under Miranda's eyes there were mauve patches, covered over with expensive creamy foundation.

'As this is my twenty-first birthday party,' said Miranda, 'I really ought to dance. Johnny?'

Johnny looked up at once.

Alice sat back on the graceful, uncomfortable sofa. For a short while she thought of nothing at all. Then she suddenly caught sight of Anatole in conversation with the pretty débutante: she noticed the light falling on his white hair and greenish-black, over-large tailcoat, and on Tuffy's exquisite dress and careful waves of chestnut hair. Then there were the pools of light on the carpet, and gleams of light on the edges of the curtains and furniture, and the charming wealthy people dotted round about. Eagerly Alice planned a composition, a detailed watercolour centered round Anatole's little figure and the illuminated carpet at his feet. She wondered whether or not she should include Miranda in this painting, and then she ceased to think of her work and laid her aching head on her hand.

'I say, you don't look well,' said a young man suddenly.

'Too much champagne, that's all,' smiled Alice.

'Mind if I sit here?' he said.

They talked.

An hour later Miranda, who disliked dancing, was still dancing and chatting cheerfully downstairs. Her tired eyes seemed brighter above her flushed cheeks. She paused only to be kind to little Finola, to introduce her to quite a handsome boy who in the end talked to Finola for five minutes before someone else claimed his attention.

Miranda saw that Liza was still seated by the wall. She was talking to a small, thin, very blond man in early middle age. Miranda laughed.

'I should have introduced them earlier,' she remarked to Finola as she passed her, pointing.

'Who is he?' said Finola.

'A baronet,' smiled Miranda, 'a dreamy classical pedant. I can't stand him.'

'Liza looks happy.'

'Exactly. Are you all right, darling?' Miranda said as she drifted on to the dance floor with Henri de Saint-Gaël.

'Fine,' called Finola, 'here's Edward.'

She got Edward to dance with her.

Liza and Sir George Mackenzie got up bravely to join the dancing. They were still discussing lyric poetry. After they found that they were in agreement on the subject, they were silent for a while. Then Sir George, carefully looking at his feet, muttered: 'I wonder, Miss Brécu, if you'd care to lunch with me on Tuesday or Wednesday?'

'Yes, yes I'd like that. Tuesday.'

He looked into her face and smiled radiantly.

'Good,' he said, and straightened his expression again, and asked her what she thought of James Joyce.

Leaving Anatole to amuse Miranda's friends upstairs, Alice went down to the ballroom. She danced with the young man who had spoken to her in the little sitting room.

It was now one o'clock in the morning. The ballroom was still crowded, but only the more energetic guests were now dancing. Most were sitting or standing round the edges of the room, or had moved on into the supper room or the drawing room.

Thomas Pagett was still in the smoking room. He had been drinking whisky steadily since half-past ten and had just lost forty pounds at cards. Shaking a little, he got up from the table and crossed the hall. After a brief visit to the portico he returned to the smoking room. He stood in the doorway. He heard the noise from the ballroom and looked through the open gilded doors into the throng. He saw his daughter's dark green dress, and then another, short dress of the same colour. He frowned.

'Got a good idea,' he called to his friends in the smoking room. 'Perfect time, what?' He made his way to the ballroom.

'Thomas,' said his wife, who was standing just inside the room. 'Thomas, you should sit down, dear.'

'Been sitting down, Flora. Get out of my way.' He

staggered across to a marble table which stood against the wall, and tried to stand on it, and found he could not. He walked forward a little.

'Silence!' he roared, and a surprised silence came. He smiled. 'Friends, ladies and gentlemen,' he boomed. 'I have an announcement to make.'

Miranda left Henri de Saint-Gaël's arms and pushed through the crowd towards her father. She tugged at him.

'Father, please, we agreed not to for another fortnight!' she hissed.

'Nonsense, Miranda, why ever not?' he said, and he looked quite puzzled. 'Friends, ladies and gentlemen,' he continued, raising his hands above his head. 'I wish to announce the engagement of my daughter Miranda to the Marquis de Saint-Gaël!'

EPILOGUE

Liza married Sir George Mackenzie in 1933 and went to live with him in a vast, half-shut Victorian Gothic castle in the North Riding. Liza read and wrote novels which were never published, and her husband collected and classified fossils, as though they had been living in the 1830s, not the 1930s. Their way of life was little changed by the Second World War. Liza survived George and died in 1977, in their castle, which was pulled down a year later. She never had a television, never read the newspapers, and only once went to London after her marriage.

Jenny was killed by a Fascist conscript in the Spanish Civil War.

Finola joined the Wrens in the war, and met and married a naval officer called Gerard Parnell, who became a Conservative MP in 1951. She had five children, Richard, Isabella, Matilda, Ferdinand and Eleanor. All except Matilda were happy at boarding school, and Finola took Matilda away after two years. In her country cottage of twelve rooms in Gloucestershire, Finola, who had anglicised her names to Fenella Leonora just before she joined the Wrens, had none of Alice's paintings save a conventional portrait of herself as a child. She also kept a period photograph of Diana Molloy, taken in 1902, on the wall in the downstairs lavatory.

Miranda married Henri de Saint-Gaël and left for France in 1932. She and Alice corresponded for two years, and then gradually the letters became less and less frequent until they stopped writing altogether, in about 1937. She had a *hôtel* in Paris and two châteaux, one on the Loire and one in

Languedoc. She entertained lavishly in her *hôtel*, and kept a literary salon. Like Mme de Staël, she received in bed. She also had many lovers. During the occupation of France by the Nazis she and her friends continued to discuss all aspects of Fascism, from Treitschke's writings to the persecution of the Jews, with equal impartiality. Miranda also worked for the Resistance from 1943. She had three sons, whom she educated herself, setting them assignments and then marking them in bed. None of the boys was particularly bright. In 1950 she started working as a freelance designer for a London interior decorator. Three years later she set up her own shop — and later company — Miranda Pagett Designs Ltd, which she ran from Paris. She died in 1975, of lung cancer.

Alice and Anatole left Bramham Gardens in 1938 and went to live in a flat in Great Queen Street. They stayed with Liza during the war, and Alice this time worked as a nurse, for the children's hospital from Leeds was lodged in the East Wing of the mansion.

Anatole lived to be ninety. At the end of his life he published some of the music which he had composed over the years. A piece was once played on the radio. After Alice died his chief interest was in his grandchildren. Matilda, Ferdinand and Liza's daughter, 'Little Jenny', as the family called her long after she was grown up, especially adored him. Finola discovered some time after her marriage that Anatole could merge into any company and antagonise nobody. He stayed with the Parnells frequently after Alice died.

Alice was killed in an accident when she was sixty. She had been riding her motorbike without a crash helmet. In her forties and fifties Alice became a reactionary, as the links with her childhood and her mother's world disappeared one by one: First Aunt Caitlin and Mr Tuskin, then Clementina, and at last Augustus. Sometimes she refused to take the Second World War seriously, claiming that the First had already destroyed civilisation. Sometimes she contemplated with drunken, stagnant horror the Nazi genocide and the twisted society which had resulted from the Russian Revolution, to which they had drunk a toast in Bramham Gardens in February and November 1917. Miranda in France chose to live in the age of Talleyrand, which was possible on fifty thousand pounds a year. Alice was content to revert gradually to a time when the great issues of the day had been Free Trade and Home Rule, and when you could not split the atom. She had need of Aunt Caitlin's legacy to do this, for otherwise she would have had to earn money by making her work conform to the public taste of the 1950s. After her death her paintings were, as they had been before it, objects of curiosity and a little excitement on the fringes of the artistic world, although in 1968 she was included in an *Observer* colour-supplement series on 'Neglected Women Artists', and that leader of aristocratic Parisian society, the brilliant Marquise de Saint-Gaël, had a fine collection of Alice Molloy's best work in her *hôtel* in the Rue du Bac.